Brooke J. Losee

THE
MATCHMAKER
PRINCE

··

THE
PRISONER
OF
MAGIC

Chronicles of Virgám
Novella Duology

Brooke J. Losee

Brooke J. Losee

ISBN: 978-1-954136-08-3

THE
MATCHMAKER
PRINCE

CHAPTER ONE

A dark corridor wasn't enough to make me nervous, but the conversation that waited for me at the end of it was. My boots glided against the dark green carpet with the kind of airiness that comes from pure dread, the kind I should have been accustomed to by now. The nightly discussions with my father had taken a turn to my greatest aversion—marriage.

My long strides made for a short walk to the end of the corridor. My hand hesitated momentarily before tapping on the wooden door. I drew in a deep breath and waited for my father's familiar voice.

"Come in," he said in a soft tone, one that reminded me of how he had comforted me as a child shortly after the passing of my mother. For a moment, I almost allowed myself to relax at the warmth in his voice...until I reminded myself why I was there.

I closed the door behind me and gave him a courteous bow. "Father."

He smiled and beckoned me to join him at the desk in the corner of his chamber. I took the chair across from him, releasing a long sigh that made him raise his brows as I sat down. "We've not even started and already you show your disdain?"

"It is not disdain for your company, but merely the topic we are to discuss."

He chuckled, his smile causing the skin on his cheeks to wrinkle. "Well, the topic is of great importance. Whether you like it or not, it is a necessary part of the position you were born into. A rather fortunate position, I might add." I dropped my gaze to the space in front of me. Guilt constricted my chest. My father had been patient with my reluctance thus far, but that patience was waning, and not by choice, but rather a result of limited time. He desired I take a wife before being crowned the next king of Selvenor, an event a mere eighteen months away and one for which I didn't feel prepared.

My focus returned to him, finding sympathy and a hint of longing in his dark brown eyes that only made the guilt swell inside my chest. He sighed. "Anaros, I'm not trying to make your life miserable. I wish for you to be happy, but you must know that this is something you cannot put off?"

"I know. It's not that I wish to delay. Only that I've seen what a marriage can be. You and mother loved each other. How can I want for anything less than the example I was given?"

A few new wrinkles appeared alongside his small smile. "Your mother and I were quite fortunate in that regard. Not everyone is so lucky, especially those in higher positions of nobility. Often our duty outweighs our hearts in this matter."

My expression must have reflected my disappointment, because my father reached across the table and patted my hand. "We have time to find someone you can at least tolerate." He tapped his finger on the piece of parchment in front of him and picked up a feathered quill. "Which is why I have made a list. So, has anyone given you an inkling of a good impression?"

I ran my fingers through my hair and chewed my cheek. I couldn't think of a single name. When I didn't answer, my father started with his list. "Well, what about Lady Ysmay? Have you met her?"

I nodded and tilted my head slightly to one side. "She's very...delicate."

"Delicate?"

I cleared my throat. "I'd rather not have a wife who is afraid of her own shadow and rarely leaves the comfort of her own palace."

He made a quick mark through the name and moved on. "Lady Sabene?"

I grimaced. The thought of being married to Lady Sabene was the thing nightmares consisted of. My father's shoulders dropped a little. "I noticed on our last trip to Dunivear that Lady Sabene seemed to welcome your attention. She's a rather lovely girl, and her family is of good blood. Is she not someone you would consider? I daresay she already has an affection for you."

"I might choose death over that," I muttered before I could stop myself.

My father dropped his quill and folded his arms. "Anaros."

My cheeks warmed a little at his reprimand. "Forgive me, Father."

He continued through his list for what seemed like hours. By the time he'd finished, every one of the twenty odd names had a mark through them. He leaned forward on his desk and massaged his temple. "Can you think of no one you don't find insufferable?"

I shrugged. "If I could, there would be little need for this discussion."

He rested his chin on his fist and gave me a pointed look. "Perhaps my son is merely too picky?"

His notion wasn't entirely unsound. Perhaps I was too picky? Not a single girl I'd met at any events over the years had caught my attention for more than a few fleeting minutes. I found most of them dull and often overly concerned with their outer appearance. Some were so pampered they dare not leave their homes for fear of their fragile frames succumbing to the uneven terrain or complexions being blotched by the sun. Even if I could get past their lackluster zeal for anything outside the comforts of a palace, the conversations were mundane enough to make me nauseous. I had no desire to discuss the newest fashions of lace and trimming, nor gossip about the affairs of other nobles for entertainment.

My father rolled the parchment of names and sighed. "It is not my wish to force you into a marriage of your distaste, but at this rate, it may be my only option. There is a coronation being held in

Zazerene the month after next. I expect you to mingle adequately. Upon our return, we will review this list again, adding anyone you find of interest." He paused for a long moment, and I swallowed hard. I suspected I would not like the remainder of his words. "At that point, my expectation will be for you to begin courtship of a lady of your choosing. I will leave the choice to you; however, not making one at all isn't an option. Should you find yourself incapable of this task, then I will make a match for you."

I tried to keep the disappointment from my expression, but there was no success in the attempt. My father stood and moved to my side. He placed his hand on my shoulder and his tone returned to the soft state I'd heard at the start of our discussion. "We shall discuss our trip to Zazerene more tomorrow night. I should like to rest now."

I nodded and took my cue to leave with a small bow. I filled the short walk to my chamber next door with heavy steps and deep gasps. It felt as though all the air had dissipated from the corridor and I might suffocate. I closed my door and leaned against it, retaining the position only a few moments before sliding to the floor.

I closed my eyes. If I hadn't found someone by now, how would I find them in such a short time? The likely answer was I wouldn't. I would not find the same kind of beautiful relationship my father had with my mother. A comfortable life spent with someone whose conversation and company I yearned for in a way I didn't with anyone else seemed an unattainable dream. Perhaps that kind of companionship was a rarity, and one I should not allow myself to hope for.

My head rested against the door as I stared out into the darkness. All I could do was make the most of the coronation in Zazerene and hope for something—or rather, someone—I could live with. I just had to find her.

CHAPTER TWO

My legs tingled, and my eyes struggled to remain open. Riding for days on end had taken a toll, and I'd never been so happy to see the palace in Zazerene. I'd once spent a month there when my father sent Captain Torilus to assist in the training of their army. I'd implored him to let me accompany the captain, just to get away and have an adventure. He'd obliged after a thorough begging, but I suspected Captain Torilus had played a hand in convincing him.

The captain took the lead a few yards in front of me, his daughter, Hachseeva, at his side, while my father and General Corvis rode behind, discussing something about training a new group of recruits upon our return. I listened to them for a few minutes before turning to check on the man riding beside me. As expected, his wide eyes watched Hachseeva with complete focus. When a slight breeze lifted her black curly hair, a half smile curled on his lips. Rhemues fancied Hachseeva—that was clear—but it was his refusal to admit it that most amused me.

Rhemues was my closest friend and the only cousin I had. His parents and younger sister had all been victims of the same plague that took my mother in our youth. My father had taken him in, and he'd lived at the palace ever since. I was grateful to have his company. Rhemues knew of my father's design to have me wed before my coronation, and he'd vowed to help me find someone on our trip. He'd boasted of his determination for days until the captain announced Hachseeva would be joining us on our journey. Rhemues had been a nervous wreck ever since.

We passed through the east entry, and my body slumped with relief. The coronation wouldn't occur for a few days, and I contemplated using the time to rest, but after sitting all day, stretching my legs sounded like a better idea. Perhaps we could forge a—I swallowed hard—courtship plan.

I dismounted and grabbed Rhemues's shoulder, disrupting his all too eager pace to follow Hachseeva to the door. "I'm taking a walk. The gardens here are the most impressive I've ever seen."

He wrinkled his nose and looked at the palace entry with longing. "And I suppose you want me to come with you?"

"Well, if it's not too much trouble. You're supposed to be helping me, remember? You'll have plenty of time for *that*"—I pointed to Hachseeva's disappearing form—"when we return to Selvenor."

"What in Virgamor are you on about?" I gave him a pointed look, but Rhemues merely straightened his dark green overcoat and lifted his chin. "All right, I could use a walk as well."

We entered through a granite arch and walked along the stone path through the center of the elaborate gardens. Hedges lined the walkway, creating a maze of dark green shrubbery and brightly colored flowers. Rhemues's eyes darted around. He pursed his lips and nodded in approval. "With a place as romantic as this, we're bound to find you a wife."

I scoffed. I knew nothing about being romantic, and I was confident Rhemues didn't either, although he pretended otherwise. We stopped just in front of a shrub cut in the shape of a heart. He pointed to it, confidence building in his voice. "Yes, this will be perfect! You just need to find a girl, bring her here, and..." He puckered his lips and dramatized a kiss that looked like it would terrify even a desperate spinster.

I grimaced. "Remind me not to bring you along when I do."

He folded his arms and narrowed his eyes. "Well, I'm not a girl, so there'd be no need for that. Now about girls. You do know how to talk to them, don't you?"

I blinked at him. "Like I talk to everyone?"

"No! Not if you want to impress them! You have to be smooth. Charming. *Irresistible.*"

"I don't know how to be any of those things. I just want to find someone I can be...normal with."

Rhemues massaged his forehead. "Oh boy. Let's try this. Pretend I'm a beautiful girl." He fluttered his eyelashes at me, and I gagged. "What would you say to impress me?"

"I've no desire to—"

"Pretend!" He stepped closer to me and gave a fake giggle, covering his mouth with his hand. "Oh, Your Highness. I'm so happy to see you."

Am I really going to do this? I cleared my throat and scratched the back of my neck. "Hello, how are you?"

Rhemues dropped his shoulders. "That's it? That's all you've got? It's no wonder you can't find a wife."

"Well, what would you say!"

"How about, your hair is as lovely as a spring morning...or, your eyes sparkle like the light of a thousand moons..." He stared up at the cloudless sky, fluttering his eyelashes again with a feigned dreamy expression.

My cousin was utterly ridiculous.

A soft snort sounded from a few yards ahead of us. Hachseeva had her mouth covered, doing her best to suppress a giggle. Once she regained her composure, she brushed her hands against her dark red dress and approached us. Rhemues straightened, the amusement vanishing from his expression in an instant. She offered us a small curtsy and smiled. "If I may, Your Highness? If your conversation with a girl starts like that, you may as well not even try."

I swallowed hard. Accepting advice from a girl in this area would wound my ego, but ultimately be worthwhile if it helped. At this point, I certainly needed it. Rhemues's advice was likely to do me no good. "What do you suggest?"

Rhemues folded his arms and flashed me a disgusted look. Hachseeva chuckled, and he immediately cleared his expression. "What do I suggest? Maybe just try talking to her like a normal person?"

I held my hands up again and glared at Rhemues. He shrugged and muttered something under his breath.

"I suppose how you approach things would depend on your intentions," Hachseeva continued. "If your only goal is to find a wife to fulfill your duty, then flattery is rather pointless. But if you want something more than that, a bit of cajolery wouldn't hurt. Girls like to be complimented, so long as you don't overdo it. Make it natural or, at least, subtle. Forcing praise only comes across as disingenuous."

I hung on her every word, repeating them as I nodded. "Natural...subtle..." I could do this, couldn't I? How hard could it be to offer genuine compliments to a girl?

"Forgive me, Your Highness, but why are you so worried about it, anyway?"

Rhemues didn't give me a chance to speak. "King Adikide says he is to get married. Given him a bit of a deadline, too."

Hachseeva offered me a sympathetic smile. "I see. So you are hoping to meet someone at the celebration?"

I opened my mouth to answer, but Rhemues cut me off. "Yes. Although, why he doesn't look for someone in Selvenor is beyond my comprehension. There are plenty of beautiful girls in our own kingdom. I mean, look at you." His hands gestured to Hachseeva, and then he froze. His face grew so pale I thought he might pass out.

Hachseeva pinched her lips, clearly not expecting such a compliment from him, and played with the trim on her dress, avoiding his gaze. "Thank you."

An awkward silence settled between us, but it didn't last long. A series of giggles filled the garden. Hachseeva and Rhemues turned to find the source, but not me. I already knew to whom they belonged. I dove into the heart-shaped shrub as fast as I could, hoping I hadn't been spotted. Lady Sabene and her handmaiden walked up the path, and to my dismay, stopped beside Rhemues and Hachseeva.

Lady Sabene's lavender dress grazed the ground as she leaned over, her brown eyes meeting mine with a wide smile. "Prince Anaros, what are you doing in there?"

Confound it.

I pulled myself out of the shrub, the branches scraping against my skin and leaving a few cuts on my hands. I brushed off my clothes and gave her a courteous bow.

Rhemues stared at me with raised brows. "What an appropriate question, Lady Sabene."

"I was just..." I cleared my throat. "How are you, my lady?"

Rhemues grimaced and shook his head. Lady Sabene took no notice, passing me a demure smile. "I am wonderful." She stepped forward, pointing at my head. "You've got a leaf..."

Her hand moved towards my hair, and I jumped backwards, nearly falling back into the greenery. I ran my fingers through my disheveled locks until I found the leaf she'd prepared to remove and forced a smile. "I've got it, thank you."

She giggled and slid her hand around my elbow before yanking me back onto the garden path. The unexpected pull made me stumble, and my hand landed on her shoulder to catch my balance. Heat filled my cheeks, and I quickly dropped my arm, but Lady Sabene kept a firm grip on the other.

"It's such a lovely day, but my handmaiden has grown tired of the sun," she said, fluttering her lashes at me from beneath her bonnet. "I don't wish to retire just yet, if you wouldn't mind escorting me for a turn about the garden, Your Highness?"

"Actually, we've only just arrived, and I think I could use some—"

"Splendid!" She pulled me along the path, clutching my arm. I'd have to rip it away to escape, and such a display would not look well coming from a prince. My father would be furious. I had no choice but to follow her lead. "I was hoping to run into you. It's been so long since we last spoke. I was telling you about my cousin..."

I groaned inwardly, and my thoughts drowned out her words. *Someone please save me. Anyone...* I glanced over my shoulder. Rhemues, Hachseeva, and the handmaiden were all laughing. Lady Sabene guided me to the end of the path, where ducks splashed along the length of a long pond surrounded by rounded boulders.

"My point is that several of the lords I spoke to think we make for a cute couple. Practically applauded their approval—"

"What?" I stopped so abruptly it startled her, and had she not held such a tight grip on my arm, she would have tumbled over. Couple? My stomach churned.

She swiped one of her blond curls away from her face. "Certainly. I find you charming. I think, as do many others, we would make for an adequate match." Her lashes fluttered, and my stomach rolled. She released my arm and stepped in front of me. "I find you handsome. Do you find me attractive?" She took another step, and my whole body went rigid. "I feel certain you do."

Lady Sabene was attractive; I couldn't deny that, but I had no interest in a match with someone whose conversation left me welcoming death. She, however, seemed most confident that I reciprocated her feelings. She inched closer, giggling. "Perhaps you need help deciding?"

She lunged towards me, and my body reacted of its own accord, stepping backwards to escape her lips. What I hadn't accounted for was my proximity to the pond. My heels hit the rocks, and my body toppled into the water with a splash. For a moment, I just sat there, droplets rolling from my hair down my cheeks. The water tasted terrible, and the smell wasn't a whole lot better. I convinced myself to stand and shook the excess water from my sleeves. Lady Sabene cupped her hands over her mouth. "Oh dear! Are you all right?"

I bit my lip and stepped out of the pond, leaving behind a trail of water. "I'm fine, thank you. If you will excuse me." I gave her a bow and a fake smile before marching towards Rhemues and Hachseeva. Rhemues was bent over with laughter, and Hachseeva hid her own behind her hand. I stormed past them. *Well, now that I've gotten the most embarrassing moment of my life over with, perhaps I can move on. Preferably in the opposite direction as Lady Sabene.*

CHAPTER THREE

My father's disappointed expression reflected on my mind. Storming through the palace yesterday, my clothes completely drenched, had not honored my royal bloodline in any sense. I was embarrassed...and annoyed. Rhemues was lying on my bed, whistling some carefree tune. Jealous—I was that, too. I wished *I* didn't have to worry about wife hunting.

After a few minutes, he sat up and looked at me. "You're not still sulking, are you? I'd like to leave this room at some point."

"You're welcome to go."

"And leave you to fend for yourself? You wouldn't last a day. King Adikide would have my head."

I folded my arms. "You didn't seem so keen on helping me yesterday. I could have used a rescue, yet all you did was laugh."

He swatted the air and lay back down. "Don't pretend you

wouldn't have laughed had it been me. Regardless, you can't hide here forever. We're supposed to be finding you a wife, and I've seen at least four carriages with lovely young women arrive in the last hour alone. That should be exciting enough to lift your spirits."

"Well, it doesn't. It would be much easier to be excited if I didn't have to focus on finding a suitable wife."

Rhemues snickered. "If you can't find one, I'm sure Lady Sabene would gladly accept a proposal."

I marched to the bed and picked up my pillow. I slammed it into him several times. His arms flailed, a mixture of groans and chuckles filling the room. A soft tap on the door interrupted my assault, and a quiet voice sounded from the other side. "Prince Anaros? It's Lady Sabene."

My eyes widened, and my heart had stopped. *Please, no.* Rhemues jumped up from the bed and started for the door. I grabbed his arm, yanking him backwards with all the strength I had. "What are you doing!" I whispered as loudly as I dared. "Don't answer that!"

He gave me a mischievous grin and pulled his arm away. "Just a moment!"

I wasn't sure whether to hide or kill him. His hand turned the knob. I forced a smile as the door swung open, but it wasn't the blonde-haired Lady Sabene who stood in the frame. Instead, a petite girl with straight brown hair and copper skin displayed a smile. My shoulders slumped with my sigh of relief.

"I told you he would believe it!" Rhemues bellowed, and the girl joined him with a small giggle of her own. Her handmaiden remained just outside the door, watching with her hand over her mouth.

I stepped towards them, holding up a finger. "Princess Elisena, have you been conspiring with Rhemues? That isn't very nice, you know."

She bounded forward and threw her arms around my neck. "It's so good to see you, Anaros. I'm glad you came."

I hugged her tight for a moment before letting go. "Why wouldn't I? It's been far too long since I've seen you." I held my hand over her head, squinting. "I think you may have grown since I last saw you."

Her nose wrinkled, and she shook her head. "I haven't grown. You always say that as if I'll miraculously sprout up a few inches." Elisena was the same age as me, but significantly shorter, and I had taken to reminding her every time I saw her. "Besides, how do we know *you* haven't just gotten taller?"

"I suppose that's fair, but even if you haven't gained some height, you have gotten more mischievous." My eyes narrowed. "I suspect Rhemues is to blame, though."

She lifted her chin. "It may have been his idea, but I was happy to assist him. You're always teasing me. It's only right I should get some revenge occasionally."

"Revenge? A sophisticated lady such as yourself could never act on vengeance. I believe I know you too well for that."

Elisena pushed a finger into my chest. "Perhaps I save all my acts of revenge just for you?"

I feigned a dramatic sigh. "Very well. If I must take the brunt of your retribution to keep everyone else safe, I will make it my duty to do so."

"Always the gentleman. Speaking of which, I saw your swim the other day from my window. That looked rather unpleasant. I'm sorry to tease you, but it was quite amusing. I didn't think my voice was as obnoxious as hers. Should I be concerned?"

"No, you sound nothing like her. I'm just on edge, and it required little to convince me."

"I don't know why you don't just tell the woman you aren't interested," said Rhemues. "Save yourself the headache of dealing with her all together."

I had...or at least attempted to, but Lady Sabene wasn't one to listen to anything that opposed her plan of making a good match. I wasn't naïve enough to think she was truly interested in me. My title had a tendency to attract social climbers, and keeping the wolves at bay often proved difficult. It also made it hard to gage whether any attention I received was genuine.

"If I knew how to convince her, I would, but she has proven exceptionally...persistent."

Elisena moved to the window, her pale green gown shifting with her swift steps. Princess Elisena was the daughter of the king of Zazerene. When I'd visited with Captain Torilus a few years ago, she and I had become fairly acquainted. Elisena was one of the few people of noble blood I could tolerate being around, and I thought of her like the sister I never had.

Her eyes rested on something outside the window, and she let out a longing sigh. *Interesting.* I slipped to her side and peeked quietly over her shoulder to see what had her so entranced. Lord Vearstram, a young gentleman from Izarden, strolled down the cobblestone path in the garden.

Ah.

I cleared my throat, startling her. "Lord Vearstram is looking particularly well today, wouldn't you say?"

She scowled. "That's rather presumptuous, Your Highness."

I folded my arms and raised a brow. "Is it?"

Elisena moved away from the window and began pacing the room. "Oh, all right. I find Lord Vearstram easy to admire...and charming." Her face contorted into a sad pout. "And positively lovely."

I chuckled. "You sound rather taken with him."

"I suppose I am. I met him last summer and haven't stopped thinking about him since."

The dreamy look in her eyes made me smile. *That* was what genuine affection looked like. If only I could find such a thing.

"Have you made any gestures towards him?" asked Rhemues. "I could see you two meshing well."

Elisena's expression lit up. "Could you!" She shifted and quickly replaced her enthusiasm with a composure more expected of someone of her birth. "It matters not. He is so sought after, I daresay he doesn't even know I exist."

Rhemues scoffed. "You're a princess. I highly doubt he doesn't know."

Elisena's gaze fell, and she bit her lip. Her sadness and doubt ate at my heart. *I'll change that. I'll help her.* "Then we shall make sure that he becomes aware of your existence."

Her face flushed, and she considered me for a moment. "No, no. It is not for you to worry about. I can manage my own affairs.

Besides, it's not as though I don't have plenty of suitors to ward off as it is." She grimaced, and I suspected she'd already had plenty of experience with that.

Elisena's handmaiden, who had been standing quietly by the door as chaperone, stepped forward. "Forgive me, Princess, but I believe it's time to get you ready for this afternoon."

"All right," she said with a groan. "The two of you are coming, aren't you? All the guests are meeting on the lawn for *an afternoon of frivolity*, as my father put it."

"You'll have to convince him to leave the room first," said Rhemues.

Elisena tilted her head, her eyes pleading. "Surely you won't leave me to deal with them all alone? You know how terrible many of the nobles can be."

I hung my head. How could I abandon her when she looked at me like that? "I'll come down, but only to defend you from the vultures that are sure to descend since your brother is preoccupied with preparing to be crowned king."

"I'm certain he would appreciate your honorable defense of his little sister." She gave Rhemues and me a small curtsy and headed for the door. "I'll see the two of you later, then."

Rhemues closed the door behind her and shook his head. "Lord Vearstram would be a fool not to notice her if she sent anything flirtatious his way."

"Elisena isn't confident enough in herself to flirt with him."

Rhemues tapped his chin. "I'm thinking we may be able to help with that."

My lips pulled to one side. "I was thinking the same. We had better see to it that he has every opportunity to flirt with *her*."

He nodded, his wide grin matching my own. "A mission. I like it. We'll see to it they *mingle*."

I wasn't sure what to do about my own mission, but helping Elisena was a simple decision. She was clearly taken with Lord Vearstram, and if I could help her find happiness with him, I would do so. *Besides, it will be a welcomed distraction. And a noble one, at that.*

CHAPTER FOUR

"Will you stop fussing over yourself?" said Rhemues. "You're just stalling."

My reflection flattened his brown hair for the hundredth time. "I'm not stalling. I'm preparing to attract a wife."

Rhemues scoffed. "Right."

"Can you blame me for not wanting to go down there? Lady Sabene will probably ambush me the moment we arrive."

He slumped onto my bed, his expression softening. "No, I suppose I can't. She is rather clingy, but perhaps you should accept her flattery? She clearly likes you."

I turned around to face him. "No, she likes my title. Lady Sabene knows next to nothing about me other than I will inherit a throne. She's never once asked me anything personal. All of our conversations involve gossip and rumors about other nobles and what color apparel she thinks will be the most desirable for the season."

"That sounds horrendously bland."

"I'm glad you agree. It might motivate you to help me avoid her." My cousin's smirk suggested he found the situation too amusing to be reliable. I heaved a sigh. "At least inform me when she is nearby so I can escape. You can do that much, surely?"

"I'll consider it." He stood and moved to the door. "Let's go. You've put it off long enough, and I'm tired of sitting here with you as my only company."

I rolled my eyes and followed him into the corridor. *Just focus on Elisena. Focus on helping her.* Of course, my father had expectations I needed to fulfill. I needed to at least try to find someone I could tolerate courting. Otherwise, he would decide for me. My stomach curled.

The sun shone brightly in the cloudless sky, its warmth immediately making my skin glaze with sweat. Rhemues and I walked the cobblestone path to the outer lawn, where at least two dozen people had already gathered. Several men engaged in archery, and groups of young ladies stood by giggling as each shooter performed and impressed...or tried to impress. A head of long, blonde hair caught my attention. I grabbed Rhemues's arm and steered him to the opposite side of the yard. I didn't need Lady Sabene realizing I'd come out of hiding.

Princess Elisena stood in the shadows of a large oak tree, wringing her hands together and staring at the crowd a few yards away. I followed her gaze. Lord Vearstram was talking to several other lords, their laughter filling the area.

I pulled Rhemues to a stop. "Go watch for Lady Sabene. Warn me if she comes this way."

He scowled. "I didn't break free of our confinement just to be your watchdog."

"Rhemues—"

He hit my shoulder and laughed. "Relax. I'm only kidding. I assume you intend to make some headway with the princess and her beau?"

"Precisely."

"All right, I'll go over there and keep watch. Best of luck."

Rhemues made himself comfortable on the grass beneath a tree, leaning against the trunk and stretching out his legs. Elisena noticed my approach and smiled, dipping into a curtsy. "You decided to get some sun, Your Highness."

"Someone guilted me into leaving the safety of my room." I returned a bow and took to her side.

She sighed and fiddled with the folds of her dress. "Now I'm indebted to you, I suppose."

I offered her my arm, and she slipped her hand around my elbow. I eased forward, and Elisena followed without hesitation. "You're not indebted to me...not yet."

Her brows furrowed, and my lips curled. It wasn't until she transferred her gaze to what was in front of us that she realized my intention, and with a hard yank, pulled me to a stop.

"Anaros!" she chided on whispered breath. "What are you doing?"

"Making my friend Lord Vearstram aware of your existence." I attempted to tug her forward, but she had planted her feet firmly in place and refused to budge.

"Since when have the two of you been friends?"

"Since I found out you had feelings for him and realized you needed my help."

"I do not—"

"Lord Vearstram!" I called loudly enough to gain the attention of all three men standing with him. Vearstram eyed me curiously as we stepped closer before dipping into a bow. Undoubtedly, he knew who I was, but we had never actually been acquainted. I'd spent the time since Elisena left my room this morning learning everything I could from Rhemues, and in addition to what I already knew of him, he seemed someone worthy of Elisena's affection.

"Your Highness," he said, straightening.

I gestured to Elisena, and his gaze fell on her. Her grip shot pain through my arm, and I barely stopped myself from groaning. "This is Princess Elisena, though I'm sure you already knew that."

"Certainly. I believe we—I—had the pleasure of meeting her last summer." He took her hand and bowed over it, bringing color to her cheeks. He remembered her. That was a good sign, wasn't it?

We exchanged proper greetings with the other lords, and I returned my focus on Vearstram. "Lord Vearstram, Elisena and I were wondering about your family's land in Izarden. It's my understanding that your father is rather brilliant and created a new system of farming that has increased productivity of his holdings tenfold. We'd both love to hear more about it."

"I believe that's our cue to leave, gents," said one of the other lords. "Once Vearstram gets talking about *that* particular subject, he can't seem to stop. Rather proud of that accomplishment."

Vearstram rubbed the back of his neck. "It's not pride. The things my father and I are working on have helped the people in our community. Why is it wrong for that to make me happy and excited and—"

"Yes, yes. We know, Vearstram." The lord patted his shoulder. "Since you seem to have two people who are actually interested, we'll leave you to it. I have neglected all these charming young ladies for far too long."

He and the other two men slipped away and headed for the archery range. Vearstram shifted his weight. "Are you truly interested? You needn't pretend for my sake, Your Highnesses."

"You're mistaken," said Elisena. "If you've truly found a way to help your tenants, then you should be proud. There is nothing wrong with wanting the best for the people who are under your care."

Vearstram shrugged. "Perhaps, but I can get a bit carried away discussing such things. I forget myself at times, boggle others down with more information than they would like."

Elisena released my arm. "Well, I want to hear more. You may tell me as much as you'd like. I can think of far worse conversations to have."

Lord Vearstram's lips curled into a soft smile, and his eyes glowed with intrigue. "I'd be honored, Princess. I—"

"Prince Anaros!"

My heart stopped. *No, no, no! Not now!*

I turned to find Lady Sabene clutching her dress and running in our direction. She stopped in front of me, fluttering her long lashes. "It's good to see you, Your Highness. I've been so worried about you after what happened yesterday. Feared you'd taken ill when I didn't see you at dinner."

I might become ill if I don't get out of here.

"I assure you I'm fine." I glanced over her shoulder, searching for Rhemues. Why hadn't he warned me? The answer presented itself the moment I spotted him. He was leaning against the oak tree in deep conversation with a woman with tan skin and black hair. I pursed my lips. Of course—Hachseeva had distracted him.

Sabene slipped her hand around my arm, and my whole body went stiff. "Hello, Lord Vearstram," she said, passing him the same demure look she'd given me only moments before. "How are you today?"

"I'm well, my lady," he answered, but his eyes had yet to leave Elisena, and they still held a look I couldn't quite read.

Lady Sabene's forehead furrowed, and I could only assume his lack of attention perturbed her. "And how is your sister? I haven't spoken to her for some time. She's such a dear friend of mine. Has she not come to the coronation with you?"

Vearstram finally turned to look at her, and she lifted her chin in triumph. "My sister is rather unwell, my lady. She has been for some time. Traveling is not an option for her at present, but since you are such good friends, I'm certain that you were already aware of that." He shifted his focus back to Elisena, and Lady Sabene pouted.

I smiled. I wasn't the only one who found the woman's unending flirtations frustrating.

"I'd still love to hear more about your farming projects, Lord Vearstram," Elisena said, her voice soft and full of uncertainty. I chewed my cheek. The last thing I wanted was for her to lose the confidence she had just gained.

Lady Sabene laughed. "I believe that is a discussion Lord Vearstram would prefer to have with his steward, Princess. No one wants to talk of such things when they can enjoy present company." She gestured to the people around us and gave him an expectant look. Elisena dropped her gaze and her cheeks flushed.

"Actually, I was looking forward to a discussion with Princess Elisena," said Lord Vearstram. He kept his expression stoic, but there was no mistaking the annoyance in his tone.

I can't let her ruin this for Elisena. I had only one option—get rid of Lady Sabene.

Unfortunately, it would require a sacrifice on my part, but I would put my comfort aside if it meant helping Elisena.

"Perhaps my lady would care to take a turn about the gardens with me?" I asked, flashing Sabene a crooked smile, one I hoped came across as charming and all the other nonsensical things Rhemues had told me to be.

She returned a coy grin, and it took everything I had not to let my facade crumble. "I'd be delighted, Your Highness."

I cleared my throat. "Lord Vearstram. Princess Elisena. If you would excuse us."

Elisena's forehead furrowed. "Are you certain you don't wish for us to join you?"

Lord Vearstram winced.

"I'm certain," I said. *But you will owe me for this.* Elisena giggled, seeming to understand what my pointed expression meant.

We left her and Lord Vearstram on the lawn and headed for the garden, Lady Sabene practically dragging me down the stone path. This afternoon would be a long one but would hopefully give Elisena the confidence she needed. Besides, Lord Vearstram appeared interested in her. *Perhaps this won't be so difficult after all. I just have to survive this outing...and avoid the pond at all costs.*

CHAPTER FIVE

I groaned, and Rhemues rolled his eyes. We passed through the entry into the gardens, and I immediately felt like a baked pastry. Zazerene's climate differed greatly from Selvenor's—hot and humid. The kingdom rarely saw snow. Elisena had once asked me what a blanket of the white powder felt like. She'd never experienced such a thing, and her wide eyes had made me laugh as I described the burning sensation from staying out in the cold too long and the satisfaction of hitting Rhemues with balls of compacted snow. I wouldn't mind smacking him with one now.

After yesterday's miserable afternoon with Lady Sabene, I'd planned to keep to my room, but Rhemues refused to let me hide, reminding me that helping Elisena, as noble as it was, wasn't the only reason we were here. The coronation would occur in two days, leaving me little time to find a suitable wife.

"Are you going to help me stay away from Sabene today or will Hachseeva be distracting you again?" I asked.

"That—Hachseeva did not distract me. Well, maybe she did, but not for the reasons you're implying. She wasn't happy about me scaring her in the corridor last night." A mischievous smile lifted his lips. "I certainly got her good."

"Are you implying that *I'm* implying that you care for her? That couldn't be why you told her she was beautiful the other day. She must have distracted you into doing it."

Heat blossomed in his cheeks. "You keep it up, and I won't warn you when Sabene comes around. In fact, I'll go find her and make sure she knows you've arrived."

I winced. One entire afternoon with her had nearly killed me. I'd lost track of how many times we'd walked around the garden with her holding tightly to my arm. She hadn't asked me one question about myself, but I'd received ample instruction on just how "out of style" my overcoat was and what changes I could make to my hair. Attempting to move the conversation away from fabrics, I'd asked her what she did in her spare time. She'd responded with the usual list of suspects: the pianoforte, needlework, and playing a social host. Why did such things disappoint me? Her response wasn't different from most of the ladies of my acquaintance, which I supposed was why I had yet to find a connection with one. Even I didn't know what more I was looking for in a wife—only that I hadn't found it.

Finely dressed figures filled the lawn. I sent Rhemues to his watch post and made my way to Elisena, who sat in the shade under the same tree I'd found her beneath yesterday. I plopped down beside her, and she narrowed her eyes at me.

"What?" I said with a chuckle.

"I'm on to you. I know what you're up to, Your Highness. Or should I call you *matchmaker*?"

"I'd have to be successful first to earn such a title. On second thought, perhaps that one would keep Lady Sabene away. It sounds far less appealing than *prince*."

"I'm not sure you can simply replace your birth title." She sighed, and a small smile played on her lips. "You may not be too far from obtaining the other one though."

"I take it your afternoon with Lord Vearstram went well."

Elisena plucked several blades of grass and twirled them between her fingers. "He was as charming as ever and told me all about his farming and tenant projects. The man is absolutely brilliant...and kind. He really cares for the workers and their happiness."

"From what I've learned of him, I approve of your choice."

She giggled and tossed the grass away. "I believe it is my brother's approval that matters, but it means so much to me to have yours...and your help. Thank you, Anaros."

"You don't need to thank me. All I did was lead you over there. You did all the rest. He seemed a bit taken aback by your interest at first, but happy to accept it. I think you have caught his eye as well, you know."

"I think you are getting ahead of yourself. We had a pleasant conversation, that's all. And it was you who brought up the subject at all. I simply stood there. One look from him left me completely useless."

"One look? I seem to recall him staring at you relentlessly for several minutes."

"Still." She stared at her feet, her boots barely poking out from beneath her lavender dress. "I hope I didn't spoil the rest of your day. I know you don't enjoy Sabene's company."

"I survived," I said. "But you do owe me for my selfless sacrifice."

She turned to face me and lifted one of her brows. "I assumed so, and I know just how to repay you. Rhemues tells me you happen to be in search of a wife."

Heat flowed up my neck and into my ears. I rubbed the back of my head, hoping the movement would dissipate the excess warmth. "I can manage on my own."

Elisena folded her arms. "But I can't? You are being a hypocrite. At least let me introduce you to a few ladies?"

"Do I have a choice?"

She pushed herself from the ground with a wide smirk. "No, you don't. Come, Your Highness. I have a debt to repay."

I spent the next hour following Elisena around like a puppy, and I lost track of how many ladies she introduced me to. Many of them seemed kind and attentive, but whether that was their natural demeanor or the title preceding my name, I couldn't be sure. Regardless, the more women I met, the more hopeless I felt about the situation.

It wasn't that the noble ladies here weren't attractive or suited for a role as queen. Somehow, I'd built a wall around my heart without even knowing, and I didn't have a clue how to bring it down. Elisena walked beside me along the cobblestone path. I glanced her way and caught her staring at Lord Vearstram. Something illuminated in her eyes when she looked at him, and I couldn't help but think I needed to find the same thing. Why did no one catch my attention that way? What was my heart waiting for...or who?

I growled, and Elisena pulled me to a stop, her brows raised. "Was spending some time with me truly so unpleasant?"

The tease in her voice calmed me. "Of course not. I just—"

"Didn't find anyone particularly appealing?" she finished, giving me a knowing look.

"Why is this so hard for me? You have Lord Vearstram and Rhemues is infatuated with Hachseeva—even if he won't admit it— and I have no one. Not one person I've spoken to the last two days makes me even want to attempt courtship."

She placed her hand on my arm, and sympathy stole over her features. "You just haven't found her yet. I'm certain the moment you do, you'll know it."

"I'm not so sure of that. How did you know? What about Lord Vearstram gives you such certainty?"

Her cheeks colored, and she bit her lip. Perhaps I shouldn't have asked such an impertinent question, but I felt too desperate to ignore the opportunity. Elisena sighed. "I'm not sure I know how to explain it, Anaros. Something in his eyes, and after our conversation yesterday, I'm even more certain of his character. He makes me feel...hopeful? Like my life can have so much meaning and happiness."

Hopeful? Right now I was feeling anything but.

Elisena started walking again, and I followed, mulling over her words. "You will find her," she said, breaking my focus. "And she will make your heart and stomach do all sorts of odd things. When you look in her eyes, your life will feel like it has purpose. She will make you hope for things you didn't even know you wanted. She'll make you feel complete."

"And if I don't find her before my father picks a wife for me?"

"Then you make the best of your circumstances and know that Rhemues and I will always be here to listen to your complaints." She flashed me a smile, and warmth filled my chest. Even if things didn't work out as I hoped, I would always have my friends and family to support me.

"I'm lucky to have earned your loyalty, Princess."

Elisena came to a stop as Lord Vearstram appeared in front of us. "Forgive my intrusion," he said after a quick bow. "May I steal Princess Elisena for a moment?"

Elisena shifted nervously at my side, a rosy color filling her face again.

"Of course you may," I said, stepping away from her to give Vearstram room to escort her properly.

I wasn't disappointed. He darted to her side and offered his arm so quickly he stepped on my foot. "Forgive me, Your Highness."

I waved off his apology. "No need. Enjoy your afternoon."

"Prince Anaros," Elisena called after me as I started to walk away. "Thank you."

I smiled and returned a small bow. "My pleasure, Princess."

Lord Vearstram passed a puzzled look between the two of us, his brows furrowed. Elisena guided him towards the gardens, and I studied them as they walked away, already deep in conversation and laughter. Elisena deserved to have someone who cared about her, and Lord Vearstram seemed well on his way to giving away his heart.

CHAPTER SIX

I whistled as I made my way down the corridor. Windows on the east side allowed bright rays of sunshine to illuminate the space, reflecting off the fine paintings and metal soldiers serving as fake guards. After meeting with my father this morning, a quiet walk through the palace halls was just what I needed before another afternoon of socializing out on the lawn.

Are you trying? Have you put in any effort to make new acquaintances and relationships? My father's words haunted me. Of course, I had answered honestly. I had made some effort to do as he'd asked, but admittedly, helping Elisena had taken up a great deal of my time. The disappointment in his eyes was punishment enough. The last thing I wanted to do was let him down, but how could I force myself to *feel?* Love didn't just sprout out of thin air upon command. My life would certainly be easier if it did.

I rounded the corner. Rhemues was waiting in his room for me to return. We would spend today *mingling* with the other nobles, and tomorrow the coronation and festivities would mark our last day in Zazerene. The thought gave me equal parts relief and anxiety.

The sound of giggles filled my ears. My eyes darted to the stairwell a few yards away from me and caught a glimpse of golden hair. My body reacted, jumping towards the nearest door and throwing myself inside the room. I held my breath, listening to Lady Sabene's voice grow louder on the other side.

"Prince Anar—"

I spun around and pressed my hand against Lord Vearstram's lips. His brown eyes went wide, and he froze. We both stared at each other, awkwardly, my breath growing stale inside my lungs. Footsteps padded against the floor outside the door and continued on, the voices fading more with each passing second.

My hand fell from his face, and I slumped with relief. *That* had been a close one.

"Forgive me, Vearstram. Avoiding Lady Sabene is of great importance, lest she scoop me away for another miserable afternoon."

He laughed softly, as if he feared she might still hear. "I don't blame you on that front, Your Highness. I happen to know she is averse to reading, so I think you will be safe here." He gestured to the expanse of shelves behind us. They ran from floor to ceiling, each one completely packed with books. The palace library had to be at least twice as large as the one in Selvenor.

"How fortunate I chose this room to hide in," I muttered.

"Indeed. And if you'd prefer, I can leave the space to you?"

My eyes fell to his hand, which held a thick leather bound volume of Zazerene's history. I shook my head. "Please do not leave on my account, seeing as how you are using this room as it was intended."

I pointed to his book, and Vearstram smiled. "I enjoy reading," he said. "I seem to be the only one, however. Not another soul has entered these walls the last three days I've been here. At least not in the mornings when I've taken the time to enjoy the plethora of options here."

I had to hold back a grin. There happened to be another individual of my acquaintance who thoroughly enjoyed this room. "It's certainly impressive, isn't it? But I assure you, if not for her father's insistence on spending time with guests, Princess Elisena would be sitting right there on that red sofa with her nose stuck between the pages of poetry."

"Would she?" The excitement in his tone, though he'd tried to hide it, amused me.

"I spent some time here when one of our captains assisted in training Zazerene's army. Rare was the day when I didn't find her curled up on that chair with a stack full of books at her side."

"You seem to know her quite well."

I shrugged. "I suppose I do. She's one of the few tolerable nobles I know."

Vearstram dropped his gaze, his brows furrowed. His reaction confused me. His entire demeanor had changed, the excitement replaced with something else. I opened my mouth to ask, but he spoke before I could, lifting his eyes to meet mine. "What are your intentions towards her?"

"What?"

Vearstram stepped forward, his body tense and his lips drawn in a flat line. "What are your intentions towards the princess? If there is something between the two of you, I'd prefer to know now. She is a beautiful woman, and one I'd like to come to know better, but not if her attention is already elsewhere."

Laughter escaped me, which made his brows knit tighter together. "I'm sorry, Lord Vearstram. I'm not laughing at you but merely the irony in your question. Elisena is like a sister to me, nothing more. Her attention does not rest on me."

His expression softened with disappointment. "I see."

I placed my hand on his shoulder. "Trust me, Lord Vearstram. That is a good thing. Her eyes have been on you."

"Me?"

I nodded, and he paused for several moments, his gaze distant. He pointed to himself. "Me?"

Laughter bubbled out of me again. "Yes, you. This comes as a surprise?"

His body relaxed, and he ran a hand through his hair. "Ever since I met her last summer, I haven't stopped thinking about her, but I'm the son of a lowly baron, not a prince or a duke. What chance do I have of courting a princess, of gaining her notice?"

"Whatever the odds, you seem to have succeeded."

"You really believe so?"

"No, I know so," I said, taking the book from his hand and

placing it on the table next to us. "Rhemues and I planned to meet her this morning and take a walk before the others gathered on the lawn, but I have a better idea."

His eyes rounded when I grabbed his coat sleeve and dragged him towards the door. "Your Highness...what...I..."

He allowed me to guide him through the corridor and up the stairs to Elisena's door. His muscles tightened when I knocked, and I kept a firm hold so he wouldn't make a run for it.

Elisena appeared a few moments later, and panic settled in her expression when her eyes fell on Vearstram. She dipped into an unsteady curtsy. "Good morning, Your Highness. Lord Vearstram."

I released Vearstram from my grasp, and we both bowed in return.

"I'm unable to take a walk with you this morning, Princess, but I've found the perfect replacement." I flashed her a crooked smile, and she narrowed her eyes. "Lord Vearstram has volunteered to escort you."

"Are you certain, my lord? It's really no bother if you have other things to attend to this morning?"

Vearstram beamed. "Absolutely certain. It would be my honor, Princess."

Good man. My work here is done. "Right. Well, enjoy your walk."

I spun around and left the two of them standing in the door frame, a wide smirk taking over my lips. Matchmaking wasn't so difficult after all.

CHAPTER SEVEN

I tugged at my sleeves as we waited in the Great Hall for the Herald to announce the arrival of the new king. The coronation ceremony had ended quickly, or so it seemed. I suspected being anxious about our mission had much to do with the quick passage of time. I glanced at Rhemues, who fidgeted with the buttons on his coat. *He looks nervous. But why? He isn't the one who is expected to find a wife.*

I elbowed him. "Ready?"

His eyes widened. "For what?"

"The mission? You haven't forgotten already?"

He shook his head. "Right. No, I haven't forgotten. You'll talk to Lord Vearstram about Elisena, while I keep a lookout for Lady Sabene." He paused and flashed me a sly smile. "And for your future wife."

I rolled my eyes. "I'm not worried about me right now."

Rhemues folded his arms. "Well, you should be. Just because we're helping the princess doesn't mean you get to ignore your father's instruction."

He was right. I had more to focus on than matching Elisena with Vearstram, but thinking about it only made my stomach knot. The Herald announced a few more guests as they entered the room. Among them were Captain Torilus and Hachseeva. Rhemues drew in a sharp breath, his eyes fixated on her. *Ah. That's why he's nervous.*

"Do you intend to make a move tonight?" I asked, barely keeping a smug smile from commandeering my lips.

"What are you on about now?"

I lifted my brow. Rhemues straightened his coat and cleared his throat. "I have no need to make a *move*. You're losing focus."

"Quite the contrary. I have mine just where it should be. You, on the other hand—"

"Shall I call for Lady Sabene now or wait until you've fallen into the pond again?"

I winced. I'd avoided the smelly water since the day we arrived and had no desire to go near it, either with Sabene or by myself.

Within the hour, everyone had entered the Great Hall, including the new king of Zazerene. The minstrels began to play, several with lutes and one with a tambourine. Couples took to the floor and glided about the room, their movements in tune with the soft music. I spotted Lord Vearstram on the opposite side of the hall.

I elbowed Rhemues, and he jumped. "What! Stop doing that!"

"I see Lord Vearstram. I'm going to go speak with him." I turned to face him fully, passing him a pointed look. "Watch my back?"

He scowled. "You say it as though I don't always have your back."

"You don't when a certain distraction is involved."

His ears and face reddened. "I don't know what you're talking about."

"Let's pretend that you do and refrain from giving it attention until I get back." I walked away, unable to interpret the words he muttered under his breath.

I made my way across the room quickly. The last thing I wanted was to be spotted by Lady Sabene. She stood near a group of Lords, deep in conversation. One of them gestured to her long yellow dress, and I assumed he'd given her a compliment. Even from this far away, her mundane words and flirtatious giggles found my ears. *Maybe she'll fancy one of them tonight and leave me alone.* I was unlikely to be so lucky. Lady Sabene was after a title, and mine far outranked most of the others here.

I stood beside Lord Vearstram in silence for a few moments before clearing my throat. "There are a lot of beautiful ladies here tonight," I said, watching his face closely. His eyes, once focused on Elisena, shifted to me.

"Prince Anaros," he said, dipping into a bow. "I'd have to agree with that observation."

"You *do* intend to ask her to dance, don't you?" I saw no reason not to get straight to the matter. The sooner I could finish the mission, the sooner I could hide from Sabene.

Vearstram shifted and dropped his gaze. "I'd certainly like to, but I don't wish to come across as too forward."

I groaned. "I told you; Elisena is interested in you. Asking her to dance wouldn't be too forward. How did your walk with her yesterday go?"

His lips lifted. "It went well. I enjoyed my time with her, and I think she enjoyed my company as well. At least I hope she did."

"Then seize your time with her tonight and find out."

His brows pinched at the suggestion. The two of them might drive me mad. They clearly liked one another. What could be so difficult about expressing those feelings? Then again, with no experience in the matter, I couldn't judge too harshly. Vearstram had expressed his fears of being beneath her social standing—a fear I wasn't in a position to understand.

Elisena was standing alone by a small statue of a lion. Her flowing blue dress complimented her brown skin to perfection and her golden brown hair fell in soft curls over her shoulders. I pointed to her, and Lord Vearstram followed my gesture. "Elisena has yet to dance with anyone. There are many who hesitate because of her title. Think how much you will stand out by swallowing your fear and asking her. Her first dance of the night. That could be you."

His smile grew, as if pondering the notion. "I suppose if I went first, I could claim a few dances with her."

"You certainly could, and I am confident she would not be opposed."

The poor man's gaze seemed stuck to the woman, deep in admiration. I patted his shoulder, startling him. "Dance with her,

Lord Vearstram."

He nodded slowly. "I think I shall."

He took one step forward, but before I could celebrate my victory, a woman with golden hair and fluttering lashes appeared in front of him, blocking his path forward. "Lord Vearstram, you are without a partner, as am I. Would you be so kind as to invite me to dance?"

Whatever food rested in my stomach curdled. Why couldn't she stay on the other side of the room? Sabene's gaze flicked briefly to me, and then she placed her petite fingers on Vearstram's arm. He swallowed hard. "I..."

"I simply must dance with the most handsome man in the room," said Sabene, giving her long lashes more exercise. Her eyes found me again. *Is she trying to make me jealous?* Irritation pricked my skin.

Lord Vearstram inhaled. "Forgive me, my lady, but I'm afraid our dance will have to wait, as I was on my way to ask another young woman for the honor. Please excuse me." He gave her a slight bow and flashed me a sympathetic look before sweeping around her.

Sabene pouted, and my insides did a dance of their own. Admittedly, I was proud of Vearstram.

"Well, since Lord Vearstram is otherwise engaged," said Sabene, giving me a coy smile and a look of expectation.

I forced a smile and offered her my arm. *Another selfless sacrifice. Elisena, you really will owe me.* I glanced around the room, searching for Rhemues. Why hadn't he warned me? I found him in the corner talking to Hachseeva and swallowed the frustration that crawled up my throat. *Of course.*

Sabene's puffy yellow dress brushed against my leg, bringing my attention back to her. The expression she wore suggested she was pleased to be the center of attention as we walked to the middle of the room. My eyes roamed over her golden curls and the silver tiara they wove around. At least a dozen bracelets adorned her wrists, and a large purple broach rested against her neck. Everything about her appearance screamed royalty, from the items carefully arranged to flatter her figure to the way she carried herself on my arm. Yet nothing in her empty words could ever bring me to court her. Perhaps her heart was just as empty.

She squeezed my arm and giggled. "I hope you are more graceful on the dance floor than you were in the gardens."

Truthfully, I believed that dancing was one of the more enjoyable things in life. There was something exhilarating about leading another person and feeling their trust in your movements. Dancing required both strength and grace, and I thought I made a fairly decent display of it, but I had no desire to hold Lady Sabene between my arms and parade her around the room. The idea made my skin crawl.

She stopped, cocking her head with her expectant eyes pinning me in place. The music started up again, and she raised her brows at my hesitation. I stepped closer, but before my hand could take her waist, Elisena's voice caught my attention. "Prince Anaros!" She stopped just in front of us, deep furrows etching into her forehead. "I'm sorry to interrupt, but your father is asking for you. It sounded urgent."

My heart lurched. What could be so urgent now? I turned to Lady Sabene and bowed. "Forgive me, but I must be excused. Perhaps another time."

I only caught a glimpse of her exaggerated pout as I rushed to the entry of the Great Hall behind Elisena. She slowed once we cleared the large archway into the corridor, and when I passed her, she giggled. "You can slow down now, Anaros."

I halted, my face wrinkling with confusion. "You said it was urgent?"

For a moment, her hand covered her mouth, hiding her laughter. "Getting you away from Lady Sabene *did* seem urgent. Or am I to understand that you've changed your mind about her."

I closed my eyes and drew in a deep breath. "You've rescued me."

She nodded and placed her hand on my arm. "And here I thought it was a prince's job to rescue the damsel, not the other way around."

"Whether it is or isn't, I'm grateful. You've no idea how painful that would have been."

"I know her well enough to imagine. I suggest you hide for a bit, just to be safe. Maybe get some fresh air out on the balcony?"

"An excellent idea," I said. "But you should go back inside, too. I don't want you to miss out on—"

"Lord Vearstram asking me to dance?" Her gaze dropped as her cheeks filled with color. "He asked me for two dances and said you helped him work up the courage to request them. Both of us decided to repay you with a rescue first...to thank you."

"Conspiring together," I said, shaking my head. "The two of you are made for one another."

"It certainly feels that way. I like him a great deal. But enough about me. Let's get you to safety." She peeked back into the Great Hall and then looked at me over her shoulder. "She's dancing with one of the lords now. If you hurry, I think you can make it to the balcony before it's over."

"Thank you, Elisena."

"No, thank you, Anaros."

I entered the Great Hall and made my way through the crowd, avoiding open areas where Sabene could easily spot me. I planned to head out to the balcony as Elisena had suggested, but first I wanted a word with Rhemues. He was still chatting with Hachseeva near the back wall. I scampered to his side, and my voice startled him. "You were supposed to have my back."

"What? I did—I do—why, what happened?" I gave him an annoyed look, and he bit his lip. "Lady Sabene found you, didn't she?"

"Yes, no thanks to you. Luckily, Princess Elisena rescued me."

Hachseeva snorted. "A prince rescued by a princess. That's amusing."

The music stopped, and my eyes widened. "I have to hide—go. I have to go." I darted past them and ducked behind one of the lion-shaped statues near the west wall. Lady Sabene had abandoned her dancing partner, who looked disappointed by her dismissal, and was frantically scanning the room. I crouched lower.

Deep voices sent shivers down my spine, and two pairs of leather boots came to a stop just in front of the statue.

"What do you suggest then, Corvis? You have experience in these matters. Perhaps you can convince Adikide that these people are a threat to us all."

I leaned forward enough to take in the man's attire—finely fitted trousers and a dark blue waistcoat adorned with gold buttons. White fur lined the collar, and he wore several rings with large embedded jewels. I'd only met the man a handful of times, but I knew who he was at once. King Lenear of Dunivear.

General Corvis, the man in charge of Selvenor's army, shook his head. "I'm certain I can convince him of nothing of the sort. He is only concerned with peace. He would not oblige in your efforts to go to war. Especially against your own people."

Own people? Why would anyone go to war with themselves?

"They aren't my people, Corvis. I want nothing to do with their kind. They can only bring destruction. Magic has *always* brought destruction."

My eyes widened. *Did he say magic?*

I rubbed my ears, as if that would somehow fix the words I was sure I'd misheard. There was no such thing as magic, yet General Corvis, a man of prominent position and little levity, spoke to the king as if there were.

"I would be careful with your threats, King Lenear. Meddling in affairs such as these may not bode well for you. *That* has been my experience. Now, if you'll excuse me." His boots tapped against the floor as he walked away, and King Lenear soon followed suit, leaving me alone behind the statue.

Magic? The conversation perplexed me, and I wasn't sure what to make of it. There had to be a reasonable explanation for their use of the word. *I must have misunderstood. I must have...*

CHAPTER EIGHT

The warm breeze brushed against my skin, tousling a piece of my light brown hair against my forehead. The moon hung above the tree line in front of me, its radiant glow giving light to the otherwise dark balcony. I drew in a deep breath. The night had been at least half successful. I'd encouraged Lord Vearstram to dance with Elisena and mostly avoided Lady Sabene. *If only I'd had one more success—that of finding someone to marry.*

I heaved a heavy sigh, poking my bottom lip out and blowing the air towards my hair. A soft chuckle from behind made me tense. I turned to find Captain Torilus staring at me, the moonlight catching the wrinkles that formed from his smile and reflecting off his piercing blue eyes. He closed the space between us in a few strides and leaned against the wall of the balcony.

"Sounds like you are in dire thought, My Prince."

"An accurate assessment, Captain. And one I wish I knew the remedy for."

"And what is it that has you so troubled?"

I swallowed hard. I didn't want to unload all of my problems on him, but he had always been so easy to talk to. The captain was someone I trusted and respected. He'd earned his position nearly a decade ago and had spent some of his time entertaining Rhemues and me with stories when we were younger. When he felt me old enough, my father had requested Torilus train me to wield a sword. The man had been my mentor, but after years of training, I viewed him as more of a friend—or perhaps family.

"I'm to be married," I said. "My father insists I find a wife...or he'll find one for me. I know what my title requires of me, and I don't intend to forgo such expectations, but I find it hard to convince myself. I've met no one that persuades me to offer such a commitment."

The captain chuckled again. "I see. Well, it's understandable you should want to find someone to marry that you can tolerate. A lifetime would feel endless otherwise."

Like marrying Lady Sabene. I can't fathom what that would be like. I'd be miserable for the rest of my life. The thoughts made me shutter. "Why can't it be easier to find someone who isn't..." I threw my hands up. There were just too many things to name. Was it asking too much to find someone who was kind, smart, and unafraid to take an adventure away from the comforts of a palace? Someone who didn't care about the title in front of my name and saw me for who I was?

Torilus turned to face me, his eyes full of sympathy. "You've grown into a fine young man, Anaros. I know things seem difficult. Even when we find love, marriage is often not easy. I have every confidence that you will find someone, and more importantly, treat her with kindness and respect."

My fingers drummed against the stone wall. "Treating her well will be easy. I've no desire to do otherwise. Finding her, however, is where I am having difficulty. I wish I could find her right now."

Torilus laughed, the deep sound soothing my weary soul. "That would take a great deal of magic, I'm afraid."

My face crumpled. *Magic?* There was that word again. A crooked smile stole over his lips, and his eyes gleamed with a secret only he understood.

Torilus sighed and placed his hands on my shoulders. "You will find her, but it will be when you are least expecting it. Just know that I give you permission to marry my daughter."

What?

My face contorted with confusion, and heat crawled up the back of my neck. The captain offered no more explanation for his odd words, making his way back inside the palace. My heart raced. *His daughter? What in Virgamor...* Was he telling me to marry Hachseeva? Surely not? If Rhemues's affection was anything—it was obvious. Captain Torilus had to have noticed. I thought of Hachseeva as a friend, but there was never an inkling of a romantic notion. But she was his only daughter, so what else could he have meant by it?

Magic. I'd now heard it for a second time tonight. Both instances had left me perplexed, and the captain had found my reaction to the phrase amusing. But what did it mean? Magic was a thing of myths and legends, certainly not reality. Magic had often filled the captain's stories he told me as a child, but his usage of the word tonight had felt different.

I rubbed my temples and propped myself against the wall. The whole thing was giving me a massive headache. *I can't stay out here forever. I should go back inside.* Just thinking about it made my stomach knot. *I promised my father I would try, and I keep my promises.*

I gave one last look at the silver moon and walked back into the palace. Figures moved across the floor, and the music echoed from the minstrels as the night pressed on. I stopped at Rhemues's side, and he gave me a hesitant smile. "Oh, you're back. I was starting to wonder if I should come looking for you."

I shrugged. "Well, did you find my wife yet?"

He narrowed his eyes. "I'm starting to think no one will ever be agreeable to you. Maybe I should just call you the eternal bachelor?"

I chuckled. "Maybe."

"Well, we may not have found you a wife, but I'd say tonight has still been rather successful." He pointed towards the people dancing. My eyes found Elisena just as Lord Vearstram guided her into a spin under his arm. She smiled from ear to ear, and his expression was nothing short of giddy. "Seems like your conversation with Lord Vearstram worked. I don't think I've ever seen him so happy. What exactly did you say to him?"

"Not much," I answered. "He needed a bit of a confidence boost, but otherwise, it didn't take much convincing."

I watched them dance to the rest of the song. Vearstram looked at Elisena with an adoration that far surpassed any superficial desire, and she returned a smile that said she enjoyed every moment of his company. *That's what I want. I want to find someone I can be myself with. Someone that brightens my life just by being in it.*

I hadn't found success tonight at the celebration for *my* future, but I had helped a friend find the happiness she deserved. One day, I would find that same bliss. *Perhaps Captain Torilus is right? It will just take some magic.*

CHAPTER NINE

My father drummed his fingers against his desk, staring down at the roll of parchment in front of him. I gulped, waiting for the lecture I was about to receive. Despite my efforts during our trip to Zazerene, I hadn't added a single name to his list of ladies, and the disappointment in his expression weighed on my heart.

"Father—"

He held up a hand, and his eyes lifted to mine. I snapped my mouth closed. Perhaps if I hadn't spent so much time helping Elisena, I might have found someone I could handle courting, but I couldn't bring myself to regret the way I'd spent my time. Elisena had found happiness, and that was worth any scolding I might receive.

My father said nothing, unrolling the parchment and placing a few weights on the corners to keep it open. My insides twisted.

What would he say? Would he pick a lady for me now? Had he already decided? The silence made me squirm.

"I know I—"

"Quiet, Anaros."

His stern voice constricted my chest. I didn't dare speak again, left only to my menacing thoughts. The journey home had been exhausting, and I'd spent much of our travels thinking about this very moment.

He rubbed his hand over his beard and leaned back in his chair with a heavy sigh. "What am I to do with you? I had hoped you would at least make some progress, but instead, I hear you've taken a swim in a pond and spent days hiding in your room."

"I know how it sounds, but—"

"And I have it on good authority that you avoided dancing for the first half of the celebration. You know an evening like that is a good way to meet new people, not to mention further explore connections with ladies of nobility."

I hung my head. Nothing I could say would make this better. I had already accepted that, but it didn't make things any easier. "I'm sorry," I muttered, choking on the words.

A hand covered my own, and I glanced up to find my father's warm brown eyes, the same color as my own, staring at me with a softness I hadn't expected. "Anaros, I can't tell you I'm not disappointed, but I also can't tell you I'm not proud either." My brows furrowed, and he smiled. "Rhemues informed me of your *mission* to help Princess Elisena. Leave it to my son to play matchmaker instead of looking for a wife for himself."

"Elisena is my friend. I just wanted to see her find contentment."

"And that is all I want for you, my son. I've put a tremendous amount of pressure on you, and I'm sorry that it has been necessary. I know how difficult this is for you, and I wish I could help you sort this all out." He pulled his hand away from mine and pushed the parchment back into a tight roll. "I can't give you much—I need you to understand that—but a little more time won't hurt anything."

My heart stopped. "Y-you're giving me more time?"

"A little," he said, his expression going stern again. "I need you to make the most of that time and put your best efforts into finding someone you can be happy with. Your coronation is eighteen months away. I plan to announce your engagement then, whether it is a lady of your own choosing or mine. Is that clear?"

"Yes. It's clear." I rose, my heart beating wildly, half afraid this was all a dream and I would wake up. "Thank you, father."

He waved his hand in front of his face. "Take your gratitude to Captain Torilus. He is the one who convinced me to change my mind. He seemed to think a little more time was all you would need, and I hope he proves correct."

The captain had spoken to my father on my behalf? I fought down a smile. The man had always treated me like family, and I knew he cared about me. *Just know that I give you permission to marry my daughter.* I shook my head, clearing my thoughts of the words I still couldn't understand. I had no intention of courting Hachseeva, but I was grateful to have more time.

My father sighed. "We have a few events to attend before your coronation. I expect you to make your own *mission* a priority this time. No more of this matchmaking business."

I nodded. "I think I've had my fill of that particular role."

"Good. Then I will see you tomorrow. Now that we don't need to discuss women, we can focus on more important matters, like ruling a kingdom."

I held no complaints about that.

I bid my father goodnight and made my way down the corridor. The setting sun offered only a small amount of light through the tall windows on the west wall, filling the space with a warm glow. My chest swelled with hope.

"Ah, Your Highness. Just the man I was hoping to see."

My eyes flicked in front of me, finding the captain dressed in his usual uniform and armor. His wrinkles deepened with his smile. "You've received a message from Zazerene, and I convinced the servants to allow me to deliver it myself."

He held out the small parcel, and I took it, curiosity driving me to open it right away. But I paused. "Captain, I don't know how to thank you for—"

"There's no need to thank me for anything." He placed a hand on my shoulder, and his smile evened into a flat line. "Just promise me you'll not forget everything I've taught you."

"You're an excellent teacher. How could I possibly forget how to fight—"

He shook his head. "Not just that. The sword is important, yes, but so are the stories. Remember them."

I chewed my cheek for a moment. "The stories about magic?"

"All of my stories, but especially those about magic."

My stomach twisted. What could possibly be so important about folklore and myths? Yet the seriousness in his piercing blue eyes left me with no doubt of the conviction in his words.

"I promise to do my best at remembering them."

He patted my face, his own filling with wrinkles again. "Very good. I shall leave you to your letter."

Without another word, he turned and walked away, leaving me with jumbled thoughts and a tight expression. I had always admired the captain, but my last few conversations with him left me questioning his sanity…and my own.

I drew a deep breath and ripped open the letter. The penmanship was lovely, each letter curling with finesse.

To my dear matchmaker,

My lips curled. The letter was from Elisena.

I hope that this letter finds you well. I must admit, I never thought I would owe you such a great debt. I've written at least a hundred announcements, but to you, I send this letter with my gratitude. Before his departure, Lord Vearstram offered for my hand, and my father has accepted. I know with a surety that this event came not without your help, and I thank you from the bottom of my heart for offering me encouragement when I needed it most.

Thank you, Anaros. It is my deepest hope that one day you will find someone to share your life with, that you will find love and the joy that it brings.

We plan to wed in the coming spring, and both of us wish to make you our guest of honor. Until then, I wish you the best of luck in your own endeavors.

With love,
Elisena

I reread the letter, my smile growing. Elisena would wed Lord Vearstram. They would be happy together, and that filled my heart to the brim. I wanted nothing less for my friend.

Whether I could find the same happiness for myself, I couldn't say, but I held on to hope. I would put all my effort into finding the person I was meant to tie myself to, and with some luck—and perhaps even a bit of magic—I would find her.

THE
PRISONER
OF
MAGIC

CHAPTER ONE

Screams echoed from the streets outside through the small window embedded in the dungeon wall. Shivers ran through my body as the sound of my people's anguished cries echoed against the stone walls. Listening to their pleas for the last few hours had been excruciating, and my heart ached at the thought of what the monsters beyond the palace walls would do to the city I called home.

What was only hours ago felt like a lifetime. I had woken with the rise of the sun and the day had proceeded with a rather normal routine, nothing to suggest that by nightfall I would find myself sitting on the cold dungeon floor in the darkness, alone and incapable of combating the siege on my kingdom. At first, the dungeon corridor had reverberated with my cries for help. I had hoped by some miracle one of the palace guards would hear me and come to my rescue. But there had been no response to my calls. I assumed no guards remained, all of them likely having chased off or killed by a Vlenargan.

The image of the pale, grey-skinned beast invaded my thoughts. The tall, hideous monsters had muscular bodies thicker than any man, and curled horns like a ram. If their intimidating form wasn't enough to incite fear, their black menacing eyes and razor sharp talons would do the trick. My hand subconsciously moved to my arm. I'd come face to face with several of them when the fight began and one had sunk its claws into my skin as it dragged me through the palace corridors. I pulled up the sleeve of my white shirt to check the damage. There was little left to see of the deep cut—only a faint scar remained as evidence the assault had ever taken place. That was the way it was with magic, or so I'd come to understand after my first encounter with the evil witch responsible for my kingdom's current predicament.

The cut along my arm wasn't the only wound I'd received over the course of the evening. The same Vlenargan had also hurled my body against the palace wall, leaving me with a massive headache that throbbed like someone was repeatedly beating me with a thick, wooden club. Besides that, the evil witch herself had taken the time to inflict as much bodily pain as she could: a cut across my face and a set of broken ribs, both of which she had subsequently healed before instructing the Vlenargan to throw me into the dungeon. *After all, I can't suffer for eternity if I die of flesh wounds and broken bones.*

All the pain had completely subsided with her spell. A few

moments of blue light ended my physical pain. Emotional pain, however, was a different story. I shook my head at the memories attempting to force their way into my mind. Right now, the last thing I wanted was to relive those moments leading up to my imprisonment. I knew I couldn't keep the memories at bay indefinitely, but I was certain giving my focus to something else would provide enough of a distraction for the time being.

I forced myself to stand. My lower half had gone a little numb from sitting on the cold floor, but the tingling dulled once I started moving. I made a slow lap around my small cell. My eyes darted over every detail of my new confinement. White marble lined the walls, stacked like bricks and mortared together. *No chance of breaking through that.*

I turned to face the north wall. My first instinct had been to escape through the square window in the center, but my attempts to push my body through the small opening had been a complete failure. *A second try?* It seemed worth the effort, and I didn't have anything better to do.

I stopped just below the window and listened for a moment, staring up through the hole and into the starry sky above. I could still hear the screams. They rang through the city like the toll of loud brass bells, echoing through the window and sending another wave of chills across my skin. I cupped my hands over my ears and drew in a deep breath. It was difficult to push their cries from my mind. It was hard to focus.

I turned my attention back to the stone wall. The window was about twelve feet from the ground, and I would have to climb the wall to reach it. My fingers gripped the small ledge between the bricks where some mortar had fallen away. It was nearly impossible to pull my body off the ground. My black boots slid along the walls. The tips dug against it, searching for any spot I could use to secure my footing. With a great deal of effort, I finally reached the base of the small window. I used my arms and elbows to hold myself up and peer out into the night air.

I forced my body forward to see how far I could go. Not far. I could barely fit my head through the bars. Any effort to squeeze my whole body through would be pointless. I tried to reposition myself, but my boots slipped from their hold, almost sending me down to the dirt floor. My fingers gripped so tightly on the edge they throbbed.

I pulled myself back up so I could peer out into the darkness. The moon hung just out of my view, but its light still provided me with enough visibility to see the shadowy figures moving across the street. Half a dozen Vlenargans growled as they pushed people along the cobblestone path, bearing sets of large incisors anytime someone refused to cooperate. An occasional scream would sound when a beast became more aggressive in response to disobedience.

A low growl rumbled from right beside the window and made my heart jump. A Vlenargan walked along the dungeon wall, tugging a screaming woman behind it. My nose scrunched. The proximity to the beast had sent a wave of putrid stench into my nostrils. Vlenargans were disgusting creatures and carried the foulest of body odors. Right now the city reeked like rotting animal corpses baking in a noonday heat.

I focused on everything happening just outside of my reach. It pained me to see how much my people were already suffering at the hands of the evil witch and her army of monsters. As the realization of how little I could do to stop the destruction sunk in, an overwhelming sense of hopelessness filled my mind. *A prince in the dungeon does no good for his people.*

The loud squeak of my cell door echoed through the dungeon. I didn't even have time to look over my shoulder before a beast grasped the back of my overcoat and yanked my body from the wall. Its sharp claws poked into my arm, and I groaned. The Vlenargan slammed me against the wall below the window, its other hand wrapping loosely around my throat. Both of my hands gripped tightly onto its claws, and I attempted to pry them from my neck to no avail, gasping as its fingers squeezed against my skin.

The beast leaned in close to me, its hot breath on my skin as it snarled, warning me with its low growls. My gasps only increased my exposure to the stench that now filled my cell and my stomach roiled with each breath I attempted. After a few moments, the Vlenargan threw me to the floor and my body rolled across the dirt, kicking up a cloud of dust.

It had moved out of my cell by the time I propped my body up with my arms. Its beady black eyes stared at me as it slammed the metal door closed and clicked the lock in place. For a moment, our eyes locked on each other.

I bunched my eyebrows, muttering through my gasps. "You know, a simple 'get off the wall' would have sufficed." The beast took orders from the witch, but I had no idea if it could understand *me.*

The Vlenargan answered with a grumbling growl as it bore its teeth. The sound made me shudder. I knew it would like nothing more than to rip the limbs from my body, or perhaps even eat me, but it was under strict orders to let me live.

It turned and left the dungeon corridor, taking its wretched smell along with it as it stomped out of sight. Once again, I was alone in my prison cell. I held my arm out in front of me, turning it so I could examine the fresh, bloody puncture wounds. *Could be worse. A lot worse.* Compared to the way the rest of my night had gone, this seemed like nothing.

I stood and walked towards the metal bars of the cell door. My hand gripped the long, flat pieces as I pushed my forehead against them to peer down the long walkway. I'd only been in the palace dungeon a handful of times, unbeknownst to my father, who insisted I had no reason to come down here. He had been right, of course, but that had never stopped me as a child. There was something adventurous about the place, or at least, there had been. Actually being locked away and pretending to be were two very different things.

I tried to make out the unfamiliar details in the darkness. There was a row of cells on each side of the prison, mine being at the very end of the corridor. A marble wall divided each cell, making it impossible for me to see into the one adjacent to me.

I pushed my hands between the bars and played with the lock for several minutes. I didn't know why I bothered. Without a key, there was no way for me to open the lock responsible for my confinement. Sorrow swept over me. *There's no way for me to get out of this...no way to help my people.* For a moment, I rested my forehead against the cold metal and closed my eyes. *It was our duty to protect them. It was our responsibility, and we failed.*

As much as I hated myself for what had befallen my people, I knew there was nothing more I could have done. The evil witch, Eradoma, had taken Selvenor over. Darkness pulsed from her with so much intensity it was almost tangible. She and the Vlenargans had slaughtered countless innocent lives today, and I was certain her crusade was only just beginning.

Magic—I'd never imagined it was real. I never would have believed the stories I'd heard since I was a young boy would turn into reality. I had thought magic was something from myths and legends—a figment of a storyteller's imagination—but I now knew that wasn't true. Everything Captain Torilus had said about the witch who desired to exact her vengeance on mankind was true. She was here, and my people were subject to her lust for power.

Eradoma had eradicated a large portion of our army with practically no resistance. No one could stand against the magical energy she wielded, at least no one I knew. I couldn't help but wonder what had become of the people I cared about. Were General Corvis and Captain Torilus still fighting against her? Would they stand any chance when faced with not only magic but also an army of monsters?

The questions haunted me, but that's exactly what Eradoma wanted. She'd chosen to not kill me when the Vlenargan dragged me into the Great Hall. She'd chosen to use her magic to inflict pain, only to heal me minutes later. And for what reason? She wanted me to suffer. She relished in the anguish of mankind. And so, she cursed me with an endless life of knowing my people would be subjugated to her power. I would forever remain the same as I was now, forced to live with the fact that I had failed to protect my people from her wrath.

I moved to the back of my cell and leaned against the marble wall below the window. I slid down the rough stone until I hit the dirt floor. The screams outside the window brought stinging tears to my eyes and my body trembled in the trickle of moonlight from above. The last of my hope waned. I could feel it leave my body like the air left my lungs.

Eternity. Immortality.

Eradoma's words haunted me and there was nothing I could do to stop them.

CHAPTER TWO

Sunlight filled the center of the cell until only the corners remained in shadow. *Noon.* Not that keeping track of time really meant anything to me. Still, I welcomed anything that could make the hours have a sense of normalcy. A small smile crept across my face. *I slept in today.* My chest rumbled with a deep chuckled as I rose from my cot and stretched my arms above my head. I rubbed my back, wincing when my hands met a few sore spots. Sleeping on a hard cot for nights on end was taking a toll on my body.

I faced the window for several minutes, staring longingly at the bright light and listening to the sounds of wagons moving across the cobblestone streets of Selvenor. I closed my eyes. The warmth of the sun felt good on my skin. I felt rejuvenated, or at least as close to the feeling as I could get living in a cold, damp dungeon.

My shoulders slumped with my heavy sigh. "Another day. Well, what's on the agenda?"

I moved towards the east wall and picked up a long, slender piece of marble. It had fallen from a portion of the wall that was cracked. I'd been using it to mark my days of imprisonment with short little lines. I placed the rock beside a single line, leaving a trail of white powder behind as I added the second tally.

I stepped back, my eyes darting over the streaks as I counted in my head. *One hundred eighty-two.* I bunched my brows. This was my second set of tallies. The first column, where I'd already made a full set of three hundred sixty-five marks, was to the left of it. I'd now been a resident of the dungeon for eighteen months.

I extended my bottom lip out further than the top and blew upward so the hair in front of my eyes would move. "All right. Well, I guess that's done." My eyes darted around my cell. Day in, day out, there wasn't much to do in my small square, entrapped by marble walls and a set of metal bars. But today would be slightly better.

Every six months, a Vlenargan would pull me from my cell and yank me off to the bathhouse. Eradoma kept me her prisoner, but that didn't mean she left me to rot. Besides a regular bathing schedule, they gave me two decent meals a day and the occasional pair of clean clothing to change into. I suspected Eradoma wanted to keep me in fair health. After all, I couldn't suffer for eternity if she didn't.

"So, calendar updated...and a bath. Today is going to be an exciting day." I laughed at my own sarcasm. I imagined the prisoners listening to me on the other side of the wall probably thought I had gone mad. Maybe they were right?

I sat down on the dirt floor and leaned against the iron bars of my cell door. I'd slept long past breakfast. Once a Vlenargan noticed I was awake, it would bring me something to eat. Such was my routine in the dungeon. I hated to admit it, but after a few months, I'd grown used to the situation. There were no options for escaping, not with the secured ward lock and the constant patrol of Vlenargans. I wouldn't stand a chance of outrunning one of them inside the narrow dungeon corridor. Even if I did, I'd never make it beyond the palace without one of them catching me.

A low snarl echoed down the hall. My lips curled into a crooked smile. The loud thumps against the floor stopped just behind me and the monster's foul stench filled my nose. I held my breath for a moment, then slowly allowed myself to breathe in the putrid odor. It still made my stomach curl, but I'd learned that if I gave myself small gasps of exposure, eventually I would become numb to it.

"Good morning, Gruesome," I said, still smiling.

The beast responded with another low growl.

"And how are we today, Gruesome? I'm sorry for having slept so late. Busy night. You know how it is. Can't seem to stop partying."

The Vlenargan only snarled. I didn't know how much of my words the thing understood, but in the dismal life of a prisoner, my options for entertainment were few. So, I'd taken to naming the beasts. They all looked similar, and it had taken me awhile to tell them apart. Now, I could differentiate between them based on their growls and snarls alone. I'd become particularly acquainted with Gruesome, the Vlenargan who seemed generally responsible for my wellbeing, if you could call it that.

Gruesome was easy to pick out from the many Vlenargans who patrolled the dungeon and surrounding corridors. It had scars across its eye, three long lines I guessed had come from a set of claws. Once, I'd asked it what made it so ugly, to which it replied with a long series of grunts and growls that I didn't understand. I liked to imagine the beast had told me the entire story: a battle for leadership or, perhaps, a dispute between it and a fellow Vlenargan. I always pictured Gruesome having been victorious, proudly displaying his battle scar for his Vlenargan comrades to see.

A click told me Gruesome had opened my cell door. He stooped over and placed a wooden tray at my side, gave me one low growl, and exited the cell, the lock clicking once again. The meal was decent: eggs, bread and jam, and even two strips of bacon. Every meal Gruesome brought left me swelling with guilt. The other prisoners weren't nearly as fortunate as I was in this regard. The guards rarely gave them much of anything, let alone a meal such as this.

At first, I'd taken to sharing the bounty of each meal with anyone within reach. The Vlenargans, however, soon caught on to my charity and had since started hovering over me every time I ate, keeping a watchful eye and giving me warning growls if I offered to share. I could feel Gruesome's hot breath flowing down over me as I started with the bacon.

"Do you know what today is, Gruesome?" I asked, shoving the whole piece into my mouth. "It's bath day." I swallowed and looked over my shoulder so I could meet his black eyes. "You should consider utilizing the day yourself."

Gruesome grunted and twitched its nose. I continued as I moved on to the eggs. "I'm just saying, a quick bath could do wonders for you. Have you ever had one? You might find you actually enjoy it if you give it a go."

After a few minutes, I had finished my meal. I stared down at the empty tray, my stomach content, although not necessarily full. There had been a time several months ago that I stopped eating altogether. The overwhelming despair of my eternal suffering had led me to believe death would be a far better option than living in this nightmare. For a solid five days, I'd refused to eat or drink anything. My body had become weak, and I could feel the life draining out of me as I succumbed to the consequences of my choice.

The world around me had blurred into a haze. I knew my time was close. But then *she* paid me a visit. Eradoma had no intention of allowing me to take fate into my own hands and end my life. With the wave of her hand, my body had returned to its normal state, and it was as though I'd never withheld sustenance from myself at all. She, of course, found the attempt amusing, and I could still hear her chilling cackle resonate across my mind.

I realized then she would never allow me to just die. No, she would see to it I remained healthy and lived an abnormally long and painful life. So, I decided making myself suffer more was pointless and accepting my fate was the only choice I really had. It did no good to starve myself just to have Eradoma fix it with a quick flick of her magic.

The cell door creaked open again and Gruesome stooped to pick up my now empty tray. In seconds, he stomped back down the dungeon corridor and up the stairs. I closed my eyes.

I wonder what Rhemues is doing right now? I'll bet he's still trying to impress Hachseeva. The idea brought a smile to my face. *Probably still trying to impress Captain Torilus as well.* The happiness I found in my thoughts was short-lived as reality crept back into my mind. I had no idea whether my family and friends were alive, and the odds weren't really in their favor.

The shrill sound of claws sliding along the metal bars startled me and my eyes flew open. Shadows had taken over the cell, and I realized I must have nodded off. Gruesome hovered over me, exposing its teeth and low growls resonating from its short snout. It held a set of shackles in its hands and the chains jingled as it held them forward with expectation.

"Bath time already?" I asked, my mouth curving into a smile.

Gruesome apparently didn't find my comment funny. It dropped the shackle in its left hand and leaned forward to grab me. I held up both hands and scrambled to my feet. "All right, all right! No patience today, I see."

As much as I joked about the Vlenargans, I was still afraid of them. Their brute strength alone was nothing to take lightly, and they were often ill tempered at best. The fact that I was still valuable to Eradoma was the only thing that kept Gruesome from ripping me to shreds.

I held my hands in front of my chest and waited for Gruesome to click the shackles into place. Honestly, I didn't think the metal cuffs were really necessary. I'd be a fool to attempt an escape. The palace was crawling with Vlenargans and anytime one pulled me from the cell, Eradoma had at least fifty of them watching me. Maybe if I had magical powers like her, the idea of making a break for it would be more logical. Still, she seemed unwilling to take a chance on me being either sensible or cooperative.

Gruesome grabbed the short chain that linked the shackles and yanked me down the dungeon corridor. There were eight cells to either side, all the same size and shape, and those on the north end each had their own little square window. I counted the number of bodies as Gruesome pulled me to the dungeon entrance. *Three there...one here...* There were about a dozen altogether, a smaller amount than the typical residency.

About a month ago, Eradoma had ordered a purge of the prisoners. When the cells became too full, as they often did, they would hold a public execution. They would dispose of everyone in the dungeon—everyone but me. All the neighboring cells would become empty and she would start anew, filling them with anyone she found breaking her ridiculous laws or suspected of rebellious activity. It had become an unending loop of death. Being thrown into the dungeon was a guarantee of one's final days, and death was the only way anyone ever escaped the dark abyss below the palace corridors.

Gruesome gave a hard yank and pulled me up the stairs. The

metal dug into my wrists. Another Vlenargan snarled at the top of the stairs, baring its teeth at me as Gruesome led me past.

"Good to see you, Crackhorn," I said over my shoulder with a smile. The beast snarled louder and Gruesome gave my shackles another hard jerk forward. "Take it easy. I was just saying hello."

Gruesome stopped at the end of the corridor. He opened the door to the bathhouse and led me inside. It was large, at least larger than my sleeping quarters, and marble bricks encased the entire room with only one way in or out. A few lit lanterns rested on a table on the right side, a necessity for a room without windows.

The fireplace embedded in the east wall remained empty. Taking a bath in a warm room was a luxury I'd lost in the siege of my kingdom, along with any other privileges someone of royal blood line would generally have. Admittedly, the transition hadn't been easy.

Gruesome removed the shackles, and I immediately responded by rubbing the raw spots on my wrists. He snorted, nodding his head towards the large wooden tub in the center of the room. With that, he stormed away and pulled the door closed with a loud thud. Seconds later, I heard yet another lock click in place, the ongoing bane of my existence.

I let out a heavy sigh and removed my clothes, tossing them into a pile on the floor. A clean outfit rested on the table, the same set I'd exchanged during my last bath. The water level rose as my body sank into the tub. They never gave me much time, but I intended to use every second of it.

My eyes closed. As I allowed my body to float in the water, I escaped. My mind wandered back to a time that seemed so long ago, one without an evil witch, monstrous beasts, or the curse of magic.

CHAPTER THREE

A line of white powder followed behind the slender piece of marble as I slid it across the dungeon wall. I loosened my grip, and the stone landed on the ground with a thud. I stepped backwards a few paces to take in my work. *One year, three hundred days*. I couldn't believe I was fast approaching two full years of imprisonment, but time felt different now that my soul was immortal; it seemed to have less meaning…less purpose.

I shrugged and took my usual place against the metal bars that kept me from escaping the dungeon. A few minutes was all it would take to catch Gruesome's attention, and then the beast would grudgingly bring me a tray of delightful breakfast goodies.

I pressed my forehead against the cold metal. The dungeon corridor was eerily quiet. The other prisoners usually stayed fairly hushed, especially during the daytime, when Vlenargans would make the occasional pace to the end of the stone corridor and back again. Part of it was out of fear of what the beasts would do to them if they made even the smallest of sounds. The other was because they were all holding their breath to avoid the smell.

Several minutes went by without a trace of movement or sound. I rolled my eyes and tapped on the metal bars with my fingers, thinking the noise might gain some attention. *Nothing.* It was certainly odd. For nearly two years, Eradoma had assigned Gruesome to 'take care' of me. Its hideous mug was the first thing I saw in the morning and the last thing before falling asleep. *Where is it? Something's off.*

I spent another few minutes leaning against the cell door with my ear pushed between the bars, listening for any kind of sound, before I gave up. Wherever the Vlenargans were, it was far enough away that I could neither hear nor smell them. Other than my grumbling stomach, I supposed that was a good thing.

I sat down against the east wall and stared down the corridor, still perplexed by the whole situation. If there was one thing my experience living inside the dungeon had been besides dreadful, it was consistent. I wondered if Eradoma had pulled the beasts away for something. *No, she would still need someone to guard the prisoners. There must be a reason for their absence; I just don't know what.*

Voices echoed from the corridor beyond the stairs—human

voices. My forehead furrowed at the unusual sound. I could hear their loud conversation as what sounded like two men entered the stairwell.

"I'm just saying, we gotta be careful," one said. "We don't listen to her and we'll end up statues or somethin'. Who knows?"

"I ain't used to takin' orders from a woman," the other man grumbled.

They'd entered the dungeon now and were walking towards me. "Well, she ain't no regular woman, now is she? Just do what you're told."

I could only assume they were referring to Eradoma. My best guess was she hired them for something. *But where are the Vlenargans?*

The two men stopped in front of me. They were both husky, built with biceps as thick as my head and had matted, mid-length beards. The two of them looked rough, like they'd been traveling for a while and hadn't taken the time to maintain their appearance.

I raised my brows. "Can I help you?"

They both looked at each other, uncertain if they should respond. Finally, the bigger one spoke up, his voice booming through the dungeon like he owned the place. "The queen has instructed us not to talk to you, so don't go botherin' to ask us anything else. The details I give you now are all you're gonna get."

My face crumpled, but the man ignored the expression and continued. "She hired us to work to do some work. A bunch of us. So, you'll do as we tell ya or you'll be dealt with as we see fit."

I chuckled, which only seemed to irritate them. "You mean as

Eradoma sees fit? You do as she says, right? But never mind that. Where did she hire you from? I hardly believe anyone in Selvenor would volunteer to work for an evil witch. They'd have to be out of their mind to agree to that."

"Took us four days to get here. Came from—" The larger man sent a swift elbow into the smaller man's stomach, who responded with a groan.

"We ain't supposed to talk to 'em!" His voice was stern and rebuking. The larger man was undoubtedly was more experienced with this sort of assignment. He turned to face to me. "None of your concern. Just keep to yourself. Do what you're told."

Don't exactly have a lot of choice, now do I? "So, what happened to the Vlenargans? Why aren't they still working the dungeon?"

"The queen's got them all patrolling the streets. Now, no more questions."

I decided against asking anything else for now. It seemed I'd have plenty of time to get to know my new captors. The two men did everything Gruesome had previously been responsible for, and part of me missed my beastly friend. I wondered why Eradoma had moved them all into the city, but it didn't sound as though I'd receive any answers from the new guards.

That evening, the sound of snarls filled the dungeon again. Vlenargans moved through the corridor, dragging their screaming victims without mercy and tossing them into cells. Whatever sort of crazy new law Eradoma had put in place, it seemed the people had a tough time accepting it. Nearly every cell was full before the last of the outside light slipped away and the dungeon became a dark abyss in the night.

The light of the moon from my small window settled over the dirt floor. My mood had become full of despair and self-loathing, as it usually did when the prison reached capacity. I knew what it meant. I knew what tomorrow would likely bring—another execution. My eyes tightened at the thought. I couldn't help but feel guilty. *Failed duties of the once future leader of Selvenor.*

I leaned back against the marble wall that divided me from the cell on the other side. Every person in this dungeon was going to die, dangled from a rope or strapped to a guillotine. I closed my eyes. It was nights like this I hated most. Nights like this were the hardest, knowing there was an air of death lingering between the dungeon walls.

Whispered voices echoed from the cell beside me. The Vlenargans had thrown several people into the cell only hours before and they had yet to lose the optimism that vanished with the passage of time. *They won't be in here long enough for that. They'll be dead by this time tomorrow.* I winced at the thought.

Normally, I would avoid listening in on the conversations of other prisoners, just as avoided talking to them. It was easier that way. Being alone only made me cling to every conversation as though it would become a treasured memory, and allowing myself to connect with anyone only made it more painful when execution day arrived.

But tonight I couldn't help but listen. Their words caught my ears like a fish on a hook, and I couldn't turn away once the subject baited me.

"That's not what I heard," whispered a young male's voice. "I heard they were still at it. What makes you think the rebels have given up?"

The second voice—deeper and rasped with age—sounded annoyed with his younger cellmate. "What do you expect with no leader? Surely that would be enough to make them quit. It's not like they ever stood a chance against her, anyway. Can't even contend with the Vlenargans, let alone magic."

"I know." Sorrow filled the younger man's tone. I understood all too well what hopelessness felt like. They were quiet for a minute and then the man returned to his optimistic state. "Well, they're still alive. I bet they won't just give up. Someone has to stand up to her. I give the rebels credit. They've made it this long. Maybe they can beat her."

The older man sighed. "A fool's dream. It'd take a miracle, nothing less. Besides, rumor is they've left the area now. Headed into the forest. Somewhere at the base of Aknar across the river."

This wasn't the first time I'd heard talk of a group of rebels fighting against Eradoma's tyranny. I hadn't been able to gather exact details of who was in charge or if they'd been in any way successful, but the idea that there was a group of people still fighting for my kingdom brought me hope, or at least it had. The way the men talked, the rebels had lost a great deal, beaten to the point of giving up their fight against the evil witch. I couldn't blame them. I didn't see any way to defeat her; she was far too powerful for mere men.

"Maybe so," said the younger man. "But I can't give up hope. I just can't. I know things look bleak, impossible even, but I won't go down without a fight."

"It was that sort of thinking that landed us both here in the first place. I appreciate your bravery, but tomorrow none of that's going to matter."

The despair in his voice struck my heart. He knew as well as I did what the morning would bring. Having this many prisoners would have Eradoma giving the order. They would take every one of them to the square and put them on display, a warning to anyone who stood against her. Once again, I would be alone in the dungeon, left to my sulking as she continually dragged my people into the deepest depths of misery.

I closed my eyes. Silence filled the dungeon, a mutual friend of despair and the darkness of night.

CHAPTER FOUR

I woke to the sound of laughter, which didn't particularly put me in a great mood to start the day. Stergis had the most annoying laugh of anyone I'd ever meant. It was loud, obnoxious, and filled the entire prison for absolutely no reason. Even the smallest comical remarks sent his booming voice bouncing off the walls.

I rubbed my forehead. I could hear him and Vorgen approaching my cell, and I really wasn't ready to deal with the two of them yet. Stergis was half talking, half laughing. "You should have seen his face when I pulled my sword. Bet he needed new pants after that one." His partner, Vorgen, laughed too, although not nearly as excessively as Stergis.

The two of them stopped in front of my cell, and Stergis flashed me an annoyed expression. "Get over here! You know the routine!"

I took my time standing up, which irritated the man even more. "Move it! Ain't got all day!"

I sent him a crooked smile. "I do."

Stergis glared at me as I made my way to the southeast corner of my cell. It was the daily routine. Every morning, the two of them would come to empty the contents of my bucket, and those in the other cells as well. Eradoma did not permit prisoners to use the palace privy, so short of using the floor, this was the next best option. That also meant the buckets needed to be emptied regularly, a job I felt was perfectly adequate for the two men I'd quickly grown to dislike.

Stergis nodded to Vorgen, who's face twitched into a scowl. Stergis always forwent this part of the job, not that anyone could blame him, but that left Vorgen to complete the task with a disgruntled expression. "One of these days," he muttered as he swapped the bucket for a new one.

Stergis had placed his attention elsewhere. It had been less than two weeks since they took all the prisoners to be executed, but the cells were nearly full again. They had placed a young woman in the cell across from mine a week ago, and Stergis seemed rather taken with her.

He leaned against the bars of her cell and flashed her a bright smile. "How are you today?"

I rolled my eyes. The woman only glared at him, obviously

finding him as obnoxious as I did. However, the distraction was about to benefit me more than I had ever dreamed. I'd been planning it for two days now. Stergis became inattentive of me every morning, too infatuated by the woman's beauty to notice what the prisoner behind him was doing. She never expressed an interest in returning the sentiments, but that never stopped him from trying to charm her. With one distracted and the other literally carrying a load of feces, I saw an opportunity. The odds of success were slim, but this opportunity was the best I'd ever had.

Vorgen slowly moved back to the cell door, his steps careful not to slosh any of the contents onto himself. *I have to move fast. I'm only going to get one chance at this.*

The second Vorgen had cleared the cell, I rushed after him and gave him a hard push against his back. He stumbled forward and collided with Stergis, the entire bucket of excretion slopping over them and soaking their clothes.

"You idiot! What the blazes are you doin'!" shouted Stergis with a disgusted scowl. I was halfway down the corridor at this point, and the two men had yet to realize their prisoner had escaped.

Vorgen turned to check behind him, trying to piece together what had actually happened. It didn't take long for realization to set in. Seconds later, the sound of their boots against the floor followed me. I flew up the stairs as fast as my legs could carry me and I was quickly out of breath. It had been a long time since I'd been so active.

"He's escaped! Stop him!" Stergis's voice echoed up the stairs. The guard at the top turned to see what the commotion was about just in time to catch my fist. He staggered backwards against the wall, cupping his nose with both hands.

I pushed myself to the end of the hall, where the corridor bent to the right. Stergis and Vorgen were still on my tail, several yards behind me. "Stop!" The anger in Stergis's tone was enough to push me harder. There was no telling what he'd do to me after having covered him in putrid waste. "You're going to pay for this!"

The corridor opened into a large area with dark green carpet and flags bearing the crest of Selvenor hanging from the ceiling. I could see the door to the palace just ahead and the large window beside it framed the sunlit grounds beyond the glass, beckoning me to keep running. *The north entry. I'm so close.*

Two guards stood at either side of the door, their expressions contorting with confusion upon seeing me racing towards them.

"Stop him!" shouted Stergis from behind me. "The prisoner's escaping!"

His words sent both guards into action. I stormed towards them, uncertain of what I really intended to do. I was outnumbered, not to mention living in the dungeon for two years had taken its toll on my endurance. My lungs were burning with the sudden spike of physical activity.

Both guards rushed forward to meet me. I immediately began swinging, hoping by some miracle I'd be able to subdue them long enough to gain an escape window. Adrenaline took over. The first punch missed the guard, but I rotated my body to avoid his grasps. The second guard caught hold of my wrist, but I swung my other hand into his stomach, knocking the wind out of him. His hold loosened, and I darted past them.

Just a few more feet. I could almost taste the fresh, outside air.

"I don't think so!"

One guard grabbed my overcoat. With a single yank, I stumbled over my own feet and fell to the stone floor. But I wasn't ready to give up. I pushed myself to stand, and the guard wrapped a pair of muscular arms around me from behind.

Squirming did nothing. His hold was far too strong for me to break free, and attempting to pry his body from mine was doing little to help. I struggled against him for a few minutes until he had his elbows bent under my arms and over my shoulders. I gave up my futile wiggling as the other three moved to stand in front of us.

All three of them possessed the same build—giant muscular forms without an ounce of fat. Untidy beards and thick eyebrows partially hid their expressions. I wondered if they spent all of their spare time building their bulking forms and neglecting everything else.

"Does everyone look like hairy boulders where you guys come from?" The sarcastic remark only made the guard's arms tighten around me.

Stergis fumed, his eyes tight and nostrils flared as he looked me over, catching his breath. He stayed quiet for a moment, then moved forward and threw a hard slap across my face. "You must think you're really something, don't you, Your Highness?"

Your Highness. Those were words I hadn't heard in a long time. The dark abyss I now called home had taken that title from me and most days, I forgot about it completely. I had no need for the former title I held as the prince of Selvenor; it was a reminder of the person I once was. Apparently, Eradoma had made a point in telling the guards of my identity, likely to ensure they understood the importance of their assignment.

I drew in a deep breath, a mistake given Stergis's current state of cleanliness. "Not really. It didn't take that much effort to outsmart you down there."

This time, a punch smashed my jaw, causing little black spots to speckle my vision. Then, a few jabs to my stomach sent the air from my lungs and left me gasping as my body attempted to fold over, an impossibility with the muscular form holding me up. He continued to beat me to the point the room around me spun. Blood trickled down my face. I was sure he'd broken my nose and, at minimum, a few of my ribs. Stergis hadn't taken too kindly to having human waste thrown on him and his rage had sent him into a punching frenzy.

I came close to passing out when an icy voice filled the room. It was enough to stop Stergis dead in his tracks, not that I could blame him. The sound had sent chills down my spine.

"What is going in on here?" Eradoma stopped a few feet away, glaring at Stergis with cold, piercing eyes. She stepped forward, scrunching her nose and looking over Stergis's soiled clothes. "And what is that horrendous odor? You smell worse than the Vlenargans."

Stergis shifted his weight. "It's a long story, My Queen, but this prisoner tried to escape. I was just teaching him a lesson."

Her heels clicked as she stepped forward, her eyes studying me curiously for several moments. I scanned over her. She was exactly the same as when I last saw her a year ago. Eradoma had made a point to visit me after a year of imprisonment, but beyond that, I never saw the evil queen who had taken everything from me. But there was no forgetting the image of her long, flowing black hair and dark eyes. She still wore a deep blue dress, partially hidden beneath a black shrug that covered her upper body and appeared to be several sizes too big for her.

Her lips curled. "You allowed *this* one to escape? The one I asked you to keep the closest watch on?"

She kept her gaze on me, but Stergis could tell he was in trouble. He bit his lip and bowed his head. "Forgive me, My Queen. I can assure you it won't happen again."

She turned to look at him, a cold warning in her tone. "I'm certain it won't. Unless you want to end up hanging with the next batch of prisoners."

"Yes, My Queen." Fear kept his shaky voice from saying more, another thing I couldn't blame him for. My body trembled beneath the guard's tight hold, even though I tried to maintain a brave composure.

Eradoma turned back towards me, smiling as her eyes met mine. Every breath I drew made me wince, and I could tell my pain amused her. "Prince Anaros, did you really think you could escape? Did you honestly believe that I would ever allow you beyond these walls? Even if you found your way into Selvenor, the Vlenargans would catch you."

I jerked my body, but achieved nothing with the effort. "I'd rather take my chances against them than surrender to your power…than be a prisoner to your magic."

Eradoma's evil chuckle sent a cold wave across my skin. I moved my gaze to the ground, and she leaned in close to me, whispering. "You will *always* be a prisoner to my magic. Or have you forgotten? You can't hide from it. You can't outrun it. It's forever part of who you are."

My lips quivered as I fought back tears. I knew she was right. She'd cursed me to live forever, and that wasn't something I could escape, even if I managed to leave the marbled walls of the palace.

She pulled away, and with one swift motion, grabbed my face and forced me to look into her cold, dark eyes. I winced at her tight hold on my already throbbing jaw. "If you *ever* try a stunt like this again, I'll round up fifty people from the square and have them executed right on the spot. Fifty innocent lives, their souls lost because of your selfishness. Do I make myself clear?"

I didn't answer, but my glazed eyes seemed to be enough to satisfy her. She released my face and sighed. "I should leave you in this state for a few days. Make sure you really *do* understand."

She waited for a moment to study my expression. I trembled too much to respond, afraid to say more for fear of what she would do to me or to my people. When she realized her threats had forced me into submission, she waved her hands, a blue light encompassing them as a quiet melody flowed from her lips. The light flowed over me and a warm sensation eased the pain in my ribs before radiating through the rest of my body as she continued the incantation. All the pain disappeared in seconds, the broken bones repaired and the patch of blood below my nose becoming the only evidence of the beating I'd received.

With the pain gone, my breathing eased. I looked into her eyes, and she smiled again. "Take him back to his cell." She gave the guards a fierce glare. "Make sure he stays there. And get yourselves cleaned up."

I squirmed in some last effort to obtain my freedom, a pointless attempt with the massive boulder of a man holding me. He hauled me back to the dungeon. Over my shoulder, I watched the north entry and the large window disappear from view, along with any hope I had left of being free from Eradoma's dark grasp.

CHAPTER FIVE

I leaned against the cold marble and stared at the short white marks on the opposite wall. Today marked the completion of my second year of imprisonment. Depressing as it was, part of me had accepted what fate had dealt me. I'd given up any hope of escaping after my failed attempt two months ago, and Eradoma's threatening words still lingered in my mind. I refused to put my people in more danger. Besides, there was very little chance I could pull off a successful escape, anyway. Between the guards inside the palace and the Vlenargans outside it, the odds were practically zero.

Screams resonated down the stairwell and into the dungeon

corridor. A few seconds later Stergis appeared, yanking a woman wearing an old, worn dress behind him. I stood by the cell door, watching as he aggressively pulled her towards me. She struggled against him with her one free arm, but the other cradled a swaddled bundle tightly against her chest, a series of helpless cries echoing from beneath the brown blanket.

He stopped at the cell across from me, the only one currently void of prisoners. He shoved her inside, and she landed on her knees, her empty hand catching her body from falling completely to the floor. The infant screamed as Stergis slammed the cell and clicked the lock into place.

As Stergis turned to leave, he caught my gaze. For a moment, we exchanged glares. His eyes narrowed. "Mind your business, or I'll give you a new set of broken ribs. And I'll be sure to let the information slip my mind for a few days."

Threats had become routine since my attempted escape. I suspected Vorgen had told Eradoma that my opportunity had come from Stergis being distracted. The two of them rarely spoke to each other now, and when they came to deliver meals or take care of less desirable duties, Stergis always made a point to toss threats. Occasionally, he would go a step further, leaving me with a hard punch to the jaw or a shove against the wall. There wasn't much I could do about the situation; I stood no chance against the witless wonder with arms as thick as my skull. I'd taken to just ignoring him at this point and hoping he'd eventually let go of the resentment enough to leave me alone.

Stergis strutted off, muttering what sounded like more threats under his breath. My eyes moved back to the woman, who was now sitting against the wall, rocking her small, crying infant with a flood of tears leaking from her eyes. Times like this always made my heart hurt. This woman was probably innocent but had sentenced to death for some ridiculous law created by Eradoma. Sometimes I wondered if the guards threw people in here out of sheer boredom.

I stared at her for a long moment, trying to decide what to say or if I should say something to her at all. It was easier to deal with my circumstance if I kept to myself.

"What's his name?" I asked, ignoring the way my stomach already twisted with regret.

The woman looked up at me through watery eyes, pausing for a moment to look me over before smiling. "Bravarias. He's just three months old today." She looked down at the infant, who had drifted off to sleep, her smile growing bigger as she observed his peaceful expression.

Her love for him was enough to bring a smile to my face. "He's lucky to have someone who cares for him so much."

Her smile lingered for a moment before fading into trembling lips and sniffles. She turned to me, a fresh stream of tears rolling off her chin. "What will become of him? Surely she won't sentence an innocent child to be executed? I know what my fate shall be, but…"

More sobs drowned her words. I didn't know what to say to her. I knew the answer. Eradoma was ruthless; she cared nothing for the people of Selvenor, children included. I'd seen enough of them sent to their deaths, but never a newborn baby.

"I don't know," I whispered, trying to keep the sorrow from my voice. I knew it was a lie. The child had as much chance of living as I did of dying.

The woman took a few deep breaths and nodded. I was sure she could sense the hopelessness in my tone despite my effort to conceal it. She closed her eyes and snuggled the infant tight against her chest for several long moments. "I think I need some rest."

She didn't open her eyes, but the tears still flowed freely down her cheeks. This was a moment every prisoner had, the moment where they accepted their fate. I'd spent enough time with doomed souls I knew what she needed right now was time to herself. She'd needed space to accept what was going to happen to her and the small child cradled in her arms.

I moved away from the cell door and plopped down below the square window. The dungeon was nearly full, which meant it wouldn't be long before Eradoma ordered another round of executions. My heart ached at the thought.

The day pressed on. Because another six months had gone by, Stergis and Vorgen spent the afternoon waiting for me outside the bathhouse. Stergis was even more unpleasant today with the extra amount of work required of him and took no shame in making sure I was aware. He would beat on the door every few minutes, shouting for me to hurry and adding to his ever-growing list of threats. Such annoyances made it impossible for me to enjoy my moment of relaxation in the cool bath water and, eventually, I gave up altogether.

Another loud bang sounded from the door as I got dressed. "Would you calm down already," I answered, pulling my pants over my waist.

What are you doing in there?" The door muffled Stergis's shout, but I could still hear the irritation in his tone.

I rolled my eyes, shoving my arm into my white undershirt. "I'm getting dressed. It's not as though there is much I can do in here, now is there? But If you desire an overview, I can provide one. Right now, I'm buttoning my shirt. Button number one…button number two—"

"All right! Enough of that!" My lips curled into a crooked smile. It was much safer to get my taunting in now rather than when I Stergis shackled me again. "Jus' hurry, will ya? She doesn't like to be kept waiting."

At that, my blood ran cold. *She?* I'd almost forgotten. Today was my two-year mark. After my first anniversary in the abyss, Eradoma had visited me. She relished in reminding me I would suffer an eternity in her prison, and not just the physical one. I assumed that's what Stergis referred to. Eradoma would visit me again, and already my stomach knotted at the prospect.

When I finally tapped on the door to let him know I was ready, Stergis responded with a muffled "about time". He unlocked the door and placed the metal shackles around my wrists. This seemed to be the only part of the day he was enjoying because he flashed me a wide smile before yanking me back toward the stairwell.

Vorgen followed close behind. Ever since I'd made a break for it, neither of them took their eyes off me, and for good reason, too.

People who disappointed Eradoma often ended up lifeless corpses, and guards were no exception.

Stergis held me tight around the upper arm while Vorgen removed my shackles. As soon as the metal cleared my wrists, Stergis shoved me to the dirt and gave my ribs a hard jab with his boot. I groaned, clutching my side as I watched him slam the cell door closed. I didn't bother to get up, instead rolling onto my back to stare at the ceiling. Any moment now, the dungeon would go completely silent in her presence. Soon, I'd have to face her.

My heart raced. I closed my eyes, trying to calm myself. The last thing I wanted was to be trembling before she even entered the corridor. I hated how afraid of her I was. I hated how useless I was at helping my people escape her evil power.

The whispered voices of the prisoners stopped as abruptly as a trumpet without air. The hair on my arms stood up, and the temperature seemed to drop as though the sun had faded below the horizon. I could hear her footsteps against the stone floor.

"I allow you to have a bath and this is how you repay me? By lying in the dirt?"

I swallowed hard and opened my eyes, but kept them on the ceiling. "Unless you're going to offer me a bed, those are pointless questions."

Her chuckle sent chills down my spine. "Ah, Your Highness. Still so full of sarcasm, I see. A facade to distract you from your hopeless circumstance, no doubt."

I stood and brushed the dirt from my clothes, sending a small cloud of dust into the air. The last thing I wanted to do was talk to her, but it wasn't as though I could escape her taunting. I preferred to give her the entertainment she wanted, to get it over with until another year had come and gone.

She stood with her hands wrapped around the metal bars, staring at me with a wicked smile.

I stopped in front of her. "What do you want, Eradoma? Besides my eternal suffering, which you already have. If you've come to remind me of what my future holds and how miserably I've failed my people, then congratulations! You've succeeded."

Her loud cackled reverberated between the walls. "Well, of course, that's what I want. Why else would I keep a pathetic prince, such as yourself, alive? You're of no other use to me, beyond entertainment."

I chewed my cheek and looked away from her. Hatred swelled inside me to the point I thought my body would completely burst at any moment. How could someone be so cruel? How could someone project such evil without remorse?

"You relish so much in the suffering of others, Eradoma. Is your soul really so dark? Do you even still have a heart? I doubt it. Only a monster could do the things you've done."

The smile never left her face. My insults had no effect on her.

The soft cry of the infant in the cell across from me caught her attention. My heart stopped as she turned, the evil grin still wrapped across her face. "What do we have here?"

The woman's eyes rounded, and she hugged the child closer to her chest. Eradoma's eyes darted down the corridor, landing on each cell for a few moments before moving to the next, until her eyes met mine again. "You look a little crowded in here, Your Highness. I think it may be time to do a bit of cleaning."

My hands gripped tightly onto the metal bars. "Please," I said through gritted teeth. "These people have done nothing to you."

She shrugged. "I never said they had, Your Highness. As I've told you before, don't take it personally." She turned back to the corridor, nodding to Stergis and Vorgen, who had been standing quietly at the foot of the stairs. "Come, make yourselves useful."

"Eradoma, please, don't do this."

The words were about as useless as the bath I'd just had. Eradoma only chuckled and forced her expression into a fake pout. "Oh, don't resort to begging, Anaros. You know that never helped your father."

Heat washed over my skin. Stergis unlocked the cell door with the key he kept in the loop on his belt. The woman screamed before he even laid his hands on her. "No! No, please!"

Stergis jerked her from the cell, forcing her to stop inches from Eradoma. She continued to beg through her sobs, but there weren't any amount of tears that could move the witch's heart of stone.

Eradoma stared curiously at the infant as though the child sparked some deep thought. "Take her outside, but keep the infant. Take it to the Great Hall."

Vorgen hesitated, his expression perplexed by her command. He pulled the screaming child from her arms, and the woman's limbs flailed madly, doing everything she could to keep hold of her son. Vorgen withheld his strength, obviously torn between doing as Eradoma asked and not hurting the child. After a minute of struggle, Eradoma's icy voice silenced everyone but the wailing infant.

"Enough! If you want the child to live, then I suggest you let him go."

It took everything the woman had to relinquish her tight hold. Her sobs sounded through the corridor as Vorgen took her son away. Stergis yanked her behind, leading her to the gallows. I couldn't take any more of it. Before I knew what I was doing, my hand slipped through the bars and grabbed Eradoma's shoulder. "You're a monster!"

She quickly turned and gripped my wrist. Blue light surrounded her hand, hitting me like a bolt of lightning. Sharp, stabbing pain moved through my hand and towards my body. My entire arm tingled like someone jabbed a thousand needles into my skin. I groaned, and tried to convince my hand to release her dress, but there was nothing I could do. I no longer had control over my muscles..

I gripped my arm with my other hand, trying desperately to pull it into my cell. It did no good and the pain only seemed to get worse the longer her magic pulsed through my body. After what felt like hours, she seemed satisfied with my punishment, ending her spell and allowing my hand to release its grasp. My body fell to the floor, one hand holding the metal bars to stabilize myself and the other pressed tightly against my stomach as if that would somehow ease the lingering pain.

My chest heaved, and my entire body trembled at her feet. Eradoma crouched down so that her eyes were level with mine.

"Another lesson learned, Prince Anaros. I do hope for your sake, you take it to heart."

Stergis had returned. Eradoma gave him another nod as she stood. "Get the rest of the prisoners out of here and take care of them."

By the end of the hour, I sat alone in the darkness. My body shook as I leaned against the marble wall, a steady flow of tears rolling down my face.

CHAPTER SIX

The marble wall felt cold against my back. Water trickled over the ledge of the window, creating an echo of steady plops against the ground. The occasional roar of thunder would cause the entire cell to vibrate as the gray sky grumbled with rage. As the storm drew closer, the clouds emptied over Selvenor, dumping rain like water flooding from a broken dam. The cell floor near the window became a muddy mess as more water flowed in from the street outside.

Days such as this only made living in the dungeon more miserable. Shadows shrouded the room, and the air was cool enough I could see my breath. *It's going to be a long day.*

My eyes darted to the opposite wall. Thin lines of short white marks covered the stone blocks. Twelve years, fifty-two days. I'd contemplated not keeping track anymore; the whole thing was just depressing and, at some point, I was going to run out of wall space. Still, it had become a routine, and one I couldn't seem to snap my mind out of.

Water puddled next to me. I sighed, moving to my feet to find a dry spot in my cell. I plopped down in the northeast corner between the stone wall and the metal bars, as far away from the invading stream as I could get. If the storm didn't let up soon, the whole dungeon would flood and the floor would be a sloppy mess for days.

The tapping of boots against the stone floor echoed through the corridor as Stergis made his way to my cell, a tray bearing my evening meal in hand. Nowadays he came alone. It'd been years since I'd seen Vorgen and having two guards deliver food wasn't really a necessity. Stergis unlocked the cell, placed the tray beside me in the dirt, and left again, pulling the door closed with a loud thud, followed by a small click.

I never looked at the man, and never spoke to him. *I never speak to anyone.* Quite frequently I went months without a word leaving my lips, drowning in my own self loathing and despair. Stergis had since given up taunting me as my response waned through the years and I kept to myself, never becoming involved in conversations with the people I knew would only exist in my world for a short time.

Even Eradoma had lost interest in her yearly visits with me. I wasn't as entertaining now that I had accepted my fate and submitted to her power. Still, she ensured the guards took good care of me, at least compared to the other prisoners. They provided me meals and occasionally clean clothes, but such things couldn't stop the despair. I'd lost any hope of tasting freedom a long time ago. I would sit in this cell until Eradoma decided I'd lost all value, and then I was certain she would kill me. Sometimes I wished she'd do it sooner, rather than later.

Thunder roared again, shaking the dungeon so much that a bit of dust fell from the ceiling. Even over the loud grumblings of the sky, I could hear it. Shouting—just beyond the stairwell. A commotion that sounded like an entire brigade of guards with frantic voices echoed into the shadows.

One guard must have stopped at the top of the stairwell, because I could just make out his words. "Find her! She can't have gone far!"

They're looking for someone. It wasn't the first time. There had been several occasions where people attempted to break into the palace, an act of complete desperation, usually hoping for food or to recover a lost loved one from the dark abyss. None of them were ever successful, of course, and would wind up being thrown into a cell.

I tilted my head to listen more intently. The guards seemed to have moved on for now, hunting for their victim like a hungry pack of predators through the palace corridors. I was looking down at my tray of food, contemplating on where to start, when the sound of boots caught my attention again. A tiny figure ran towards me in the darkness, breathing hard through sobs. They threw themselves against the back wall, unaware I was sitting just a few feet away. A small girl curled against the stone, her arms wrapping around her legs as she buried her face into her trousers. I could hear her muffled cries, and the sound pierced my heart like a knife.

Don't. Don't talk to her. You can't let yourself get involved. You can't let yourself care...

I tried to focus on something else: the growing puddle of water at the back of the cell, the clash of thunder and flashes of light. I even tried counting the bricks on the opposite wall, which was pointless because I already knew there were eighty-eight. But I couldn't ignore her sobs. They pulled at my heart and there was nothing I could do to stop my words.

"It's all right," I whispered.

The sound of my voice startled her, and she jumped. She looked over at me, her chin still resting on her knees. In the darkness, there was little I could see of her features, but I could tell she was young, ten or eleven at my best guess. I picked up a few pieces of sliced apple and offered her some. I thought the gesture might calm her sobs, if nothing else.

She stared at me for a moment before burying her face back into her pants. I sighed. I couldn't blame her for being afraid and there wasn't anything I could do to help her, but I wanted to try. Despite all my intentions to distance myself from other people, I felt compelled to comfort her, even if only for a moment.

"Fear knows only what our mind allows it," I said, keeping my tone even in hopes of soothing her. My mouth curved a little at the words. "My father used to say that."

The girl looked at me again, quiet for several moments before her small voice gained enough courage to speak. "What does it mean?"

My smile widened. "It means, we can't be afraid if we refuse to give into our fear. Facing the things that scare us most takes away the control they have over us. Fear is afraid of those with the courage to face it."

The girl considered my words. "What if I can't find the courage to face it? What if I don't know where to look?"

"It's easy to find," I answered. "It's inside of you. A part of you. All you have to do is use it."

Even in the darkness, I could see her mouth curve into a bright smile. I looked away, part of me feeling guilty for giving her false hope. *Stop. You're getting attached. You can't let yourself get attached. Not when you know what happens.*

Voices filled the corridor beyond the stairwell. The guards approached the dungeon. The girl seemed to understand what was coming too, and she gave a little sniffle. I shifted as close to the metal bars as I could, my heart racing and my voice shaky. "Everything's going to be all right."

She knew it was a lie. I knew it was a lie, But I couldn't stop the words. Perhaps it was because they were the deepest desires of my heart. I wanted my people to be safe. I wanted them to be free of Eradoma's evil reign. Accepting I could accomplish neither of those things never became any easier.

Several guards marched through the dungeon corridor. "She's

down here!" one of them yelled. "We've got her!"

The girl pushed her body against the wall as tightly as she could, her sobs echoing over the sound of their boots tapping the stone floor. Stergis pushed his way past the others and clasped his hands tightly around her arm. He yanked her from the ground as she fought to free herself from his hold.

"Which cell should we toss her in?" asked the guard behind him, ready with a set of keys jingling between his fingers.

"None," replied Stergis. "The queen asked we bring the girl directly to her. She wants to deal with this herself."

I stood up and grabbed the metal bars. "Stergis! Stergis, please don't do this! She's only a child!" Stergis yanked her towards my cell so he could lean close to me, a smirk smeared across his face. My fingers tightened on the bars and my skin grew hot. "You know if you take her to Eradoma, she'll kill her." I swallowed hard. Begging Stergis for anything wasn't something I enjoyed, but if there was even a slight chance he would consider my pleas, I'd do it for her sake. "Stergis, please! Just let her go. Tell Eradoma she escaped into the city."

The smile on his face only grew at my begs. "Mind your business. I still don't mind breaking ribs."

He pulled her away and made his way to the stairwell. The girl gave me one last look over her shoulder as Stergis dragged her forward. They passed through a thin beam of light filtering in from a cell window and I could see her piercing blue eyes overflowing with tears.

"No! Stergis!"

Seconds later, they had all disappeared. The dungeon grew quiet, except for the sound of water dripping from the window ledge. I fell back against the marble wall and slid down it until my body met the floor. Both of my hands moved to my head, my fingers weaving between the locks of my hair. I tried to keep them at bay, but the tears flowed from my eyes like the water from the dark grey storm clouds beyond my cell.

My body trembled in the shadows. *When will it end? Am I destined to be a prisoner for eternity?* This was why I kept my distance from the people brought into the dark abyss. I had allowed myself, in those few short minutes, to connect to another person, and now the heartache of losing that connection filled me with the darkest despair.

I'll always be a prisoner. Whether I'm here or, by some miracle, find my freedom. None of it matters. These walls don't define what I am.

To many, the idea of immortality was a great gift. Those who yearned for power often craved the possibility of an eternal life, where they could celebrate their victories and rule without end. But I wasn't one of those people. My immortality was a curse, one given to me by an evil witch who'd taken away everything I ever cared about. With no hope that she could be defeated, I feared my people would suffer endlessly under her rule.

These marble walls aren't what makes me a prisoner. I am a prisoner of magic.

CHAPTER SEVEN

A guard took my empty tray without a word, not that I wanted him to say anything. Truthfully, I didn't even know the man's name. I hadn't seen Stergis in over a year, and now several men rotated through dungeon duty. All of them paid me no heed, and I responded in kind. After two decades in my damp cell, I'd become quite used to being alone.

My eyes grew heavy as I leaned against the marble wall beneath my small window. Moonlight lit the area in front of me, but my body remained shadowed. I tried to sleep, but found it difficult to drift away. Such was my monotonous life that time seemed to drag on. Seconds faded to minutes, and the hour grew late.

The silence of the dungeon became broken by voices, and they grew louder as footsteps entered the stairwell. I didn't bother to move. The guards brought prisoners to the dungeon at all hours of the day, and tonight would be no different.

With the prison already crowded, it was no surprise that the guards marched their new captive all the way to the end of the corridor. "Where are we going to put her?" one of them asked. "The cells...they are all so full!"

"I know a spot," replied a second guard.

They stopped at the end of the corridor, and the screech of a door echoed off the walls. I assumed they had placed the prisoner in the cell opposite my own, but to my surprise, a loud thump sounded through my tiny space when they shoved a body to the floor. A petite figure lay a few feet away from me, the moonlight illuminating the folds of their long cloak. A hood concealed their face.

I blinked. Surely I was hallucinating?

A click announced a guard had secured the lock. He drew a deep breath with his yawn and tilted his head, his neck cracking with the motion. "Let's go get some sleep. Our work here is done."

As the guards disappeared from view, my new cell mate stood. Their hands pulled back their hood, revealing a head of wavy brown curls. I watched the woman analyze her new surroundings. From what I could tell, she was young, perhaps only a little younger than myself.

Or younger than I was when Eradoma cursed me.

Technically, I should have been almost forty by now, but my body had remained the same for the last two decades. The immortality curse hadn't even allowed me to grow facial hair, and for years it disappointed me how I couldn't even sport a long, scruffy beard to match the layers of dirt caked onto my skin.

When the young woman's gaze approached my resting place, I closed my eyes. I didn't know why I felt the need to fake sleep, my body reacting before I even had time to think. Perhaps I believed she might feel uncomfortable being alone in such a place with a stranger, and honestly, I didn't quite know how to act myself. In my twenty years of imprisonment, I'd never had a cellmate. I hadn't been this close to anyone except the guards for a long time.

I dared a peek at her. She had gone back to studying our cell, running her fingers along the walls as if searching for any flaws in the structure. She moved on to the thick bars of the cell door, starting her analysis as high as she could reach and ending near the floor.

"There's no point," I said. My whispered voice startled both of us. She hadn't expected the person she thought was sleeping to speak, and I hadn't expected to let words fall from my lips. Having not used my voice in weeks, the sound came out almost raspy.

She turned to face me. "What?"

I sat up straighter, keeping my movements slow so as to not startle her further. The shadows did nothing to help. "I said, there's no point. I've been over every inch of this place a thousand times, and you are wasting your time."

She laughed, but I could see frustration spread across her moonlit features. "I'm sorry, then what exactly would you have me waste my time with? Fancy a game of chess in the dirt?"

I chuckled. I *actually* chuckled. How long had it been since I'd done that? I couldn't remember the last time I'd genuinely laughed. Occasionally, the guards would say something rather stupid, but even they had ceased to amuse me after a while. Yet it had taken my new cellmate all but a few minutes to coax it out of me. I liked her already.

I dragged myself from the floor and brushed the dirt from my trousers. "What I *suggest* is you accept the fact that the only way you are leaving this dungeon is in a box or headed for the gallows."

Her brows crumpled as I walked past her and placed my hands on the cold metal bars. Bodies filled the cells on the opposite side of the corridor to capacity. How long would Eradoma wait to give an execution order? Would this young lady occupy my space for hours or days?

"Well, some of us do not toss away hope so easily."

I turned to face her, and laughter bubbled out of me before I could speak. She stood with her arms folded and her chin lifted, daring me with her expression to argue against her words.

"Easily?" I asked. Perhaps if she knew, if she understood, the woman would not make such an assumption. I'd held onto hope for years, but it had profited me nothing. My people still suffered under Eradoma's evil reign, and I remained a prisoner to both the palace dungeon and to time.

I shook my head. *I can't explain any of that to her.* What was the point? She would only exist in my tiny world for a moment, and then her life would end. Explaining my circumstances only drudged up memories I preferred to keep buried.

My eyes darted over her face, studying every detail where the silver light of the moon illuminated her face. At one time, my resolve to help my people had held strong. I had portrayed confidence and spirit just like she did, but years of fruitless effort ran those reserves of optimism dry.

"What is your name?" I asked.

"Zynnera."

She stared at me, as though waiting for me to respond. But I couldn't tell her my name. She might think me insane, or worse, believe me and display her disappointment. I was a prince who had failed his people, and the guilt was almost worse than torture by Eradoma's magic.

I turned away from her, sliding my hands along the metal bar as I stared down the dark corridor. "And what is it you've done to deserve being thrown into the dungeon, Zynnera?"

Her response came laced with frustration. "I could ask you the same thing?"

I laughed again. How did she manage to bring it out of me so easily? This time, I released the bar to face her fully. "So much hope, yet so little trust?"

Even in this dimly lit space, I could see her cheeks turn red. "Now you suggest I trust a stranger that I've only just met? A hypocritical statement coming from someone who has told me nothing of himself!"

I averted my gaze. Her words stabbed at my heart. I couldn't deny the accusation, but fear kept me from telling her who I was. Opening up to another prisoner was a mistake I'd made time and again, and I refused to spend days wallowing in sorrow because I allowed myself to become attached to someone.

But this is different, isn't it? She's in my cell. I can't just avoid her.

"Stealing." Her voice pulled me from my thoughts, and I looked at her. She shifted her weight and bit her lip, uncertainty lingering in her expression. "Stealing food from the palace...and giving it to the people. I've been doing it for years."

I tried to stop the smile from spreading across my face, but the effort did no good. Anyone who stood against Eradoma won my favor, even if it landed them in the dungeon. I stepped forward until only a few feet remained between us. Staring into her piercing blue eyes, I could sense her hope and courage, and for the first time in years, something ignited in my soul. Could I dare to hope for freedom and to save my people?

Zynnera made me want to hope. Whether I actually could was another thing entirely, but right now, she made me believe in the possibility of a brighter future.

For several moments, she stared back at me, her eyes wandering my face as though searching for something. When the silence grew too awkward, she cleared her throat and looked away. "Now, if you don't mind, I'd rather not spend the rest of the night in this dreary dungeon."

My face crumpled, but before I could ask what she meant, Zynnera had marched past me towards the cell door. Her fingers glided through her wavy brown hair until they found a decorative hairpiece. She slipped the pin from her head, loosening a strand to fall against her cheek.

My stomach twisted, though why, I didn't know. I certainly

couldn't take my eyes off her movements, especially as she stuck her hands through the bars and inserted the pin into the lock. A few wiggles and a click echoed through the corridor. She removed the lock and placed it on the dungeon floor.

I gaped.

Twenty years I'd spent trapped in this dark abyss, and Zynnera had needed all but fifteen minutes to escape. What a terrible excuse for a prince I'd turned out to be. I couldn't even escape my own dungeon.

She glanced over her shoulder, and her brows lifted. "Well, are you coming or not?"

For a moment, I hesitated, not because I didn't want to leave, but because I thought perhaps this entire scene was nothing more than a dream. Finally coming to my senses, I rushed to her side and extended my palm towards her. "The pin."

Zynnera narrowed her eyes. I couldn't blame her for being suspicious. I wouldn't even tell her my name. "We can't leave until we've freed the others," I said, hoping she would believe my words.

Her expression softened, and her lips pulled into a small smile. My chest constricted and a wave of flutters filled every inch of my stomach. *What is wrong with me? I'm anxious to escape, to finally be free of this dark abyss. That's all.*

Zynnera placed the pin in my palm, and I shook off the strange sensations rushing through my body. I needed to concentrate. Tonight I would save not only myself, but everyone in the dungeon. I couldn't allow myself to lose focus, not even in my own exuberance.

One by one, I inserted Zynnera's pin into the locks of each cell. With every click, the hope inside me continued to swell. *I'll finally leave this prison. I'll finally be free.*

Perhaps that wasn't the truth. I could never be completely free with Eradoma's magic coursing through my veins. But this opportunity, this chance to break out of these marble walls, would allow me to help my people. If there was a way to defeat Eradoma, I would find it, even if it took me the rest of my life. And because she had cursed me with immortality, I had a long time to accomplish the task.

THE END

Follow Anaros and Zynnera's story in Book 1: *The Witch of Selvenor*!

Thank you for reading! If you enjoyed this book, please consider leaving me a review on Amazon!

Want more? Visit my website www.brookejlosee.com for character art, excerpts, and more! You can also sign up for my monthly newsletter. Just follow this link or scan the code:

https://bit.ly/VirgamorMessenger

Titles in this series:

The Matchmaker Prince (Novella)
The Prisoner of Magic (Novella)
The Witch of Selvenor (Book 1)
The Warlock of Dunivear (Book 2)
Origins of Virgàm (Book 3)
The Seer of Verascene (Book 4)
Shadows of Aknar (Book 5)
Path to Irrilàm (Book 6)
The Sorcerer of Kantinar (Book 7)

Want more stories from this magical world? Check out
my other books!

Blood & Magic (Book 1)
Love & Magic (Book 2)
Revenge & Magic (Book 3)
War & Magic (Book 4)

Acknowledgments

Writing a book requires a team, and I am ever so fortunate to have the best people by my side to help me every step of the way. A big shout out to all those involved in getting this book on the shelves—to you I owe so much. Thank you!

To my wonderful husband, who not only encourages me to continue, but also assists in making my covers. To my beta readers, Justena White, whose invaluable feedback helped me continually improve and make this story even stronger. To Jake and Mindy Porter for always providing helpful insight and encouragement. To Kaybree Cowley, my number one fan who's demands for the next chapter keep me going. And to all those who continue to support me on this writing adventure, thank you.

ABOUT THE AUTHOR

Brooke Losee lives in Utah with her husband and three children. She enjoys writing, gardening, rock hounding, and just being a *mom*. Brooke appreciates the small town lifestyle and adventurous landscapes of where she lives, often using her background in Geology to aid in her writing. She has always had a passion for science, history, and of course, all things books.